Drea—
Hope you enjoy!
Thanks & good luck
in prison.
Justin

SEASON
OF ASH

JUSTIN BRYANT

SEASON OF ASH

ENC Press

SEASON OF ASH © 2004 Justin Bryant

For information, contact ENC Press at pr@encpress.com

ISBN 0-9728321-7-3

Printed in the United States of America

FIRST EDITION 2004

10 9 8 7 6 5 4 3 2 1

Design and cover art by

AUTHOR'S NOTE

This is a work of fiction and is not meant to accurately portray any actual historical events, places, or persons. All characters are products of the author's imagination. Dialogue in Zulu has been rendered into idiomatic English. In some cases, this includes the use of English words that have no direct Zulu translation.

———

Special thanks to Olga Gardner Galvin, who saw the promise and helped me realize this novel. Thanks, too, to three important early readers of the manuscript, for their support, encouragement, and constructive criticism: Jay Holloway, Sean Carswell, and Jean Schwind. And thanks to Scott Mahan for the use of his computer.

June 1976

The morning didn't feel especially cold, but David Themba pulled on an extra sweater and a tight woolen cap. He left his house early. Smoke from morning fires streamed from the listing shanties bunched together on the face of an ugly orange hill. He saw other children on their way to Sekano-Ntoane, his school. David's small body shook with excitement and a vague sense of dread. It was June 16, 1976, and he thought something important was going to happen.

"Where are we meeting them?" Nthato asked him in front of the school.

"Vilikazi Street, outside Phefeni Junior. They might be there already."

"Will Stephen be there?"

"Yeah! All the schools, all the students will be. Stephen is the student leader at Phefeni," David said, surging with pride at the thought of his older brother. "Stephen says this madness about Afrikaans has gone far enough."

In front of the school the students milled in distinct

groups before congregating, when some began singing "*Amandla, awethu,* power is ours!" Nthato held up a scrawled sign that read THE BLACK NATION IS NOT A PLACE FOR IMPURITIES! AFRIKAANS STINKS! David stepped to the front of the children and cried, "Now on to Phefeni!" Teachers stood by forlornly as the students—perhaps as many as four hundred—rushed into the street.

They sang and danced as they moved through Soweto, and adults came from their shanties to smile curiously at them. When they reached Vilikazi Street, David blinked in amazement: here were several hundred more students, maybe even a thousand, many of them from the high schools. They sang, carrying sticks and makeshift clubs. They shouted, they saluted with the Black Power fist. David stood on his toes, searching for Stephen. He found him leading a cry of "Power! Power!" The high school students looked massive. While David and his young friends sang joyously, the shouts of the older students were filled with real anger.

"Tebello says the police and soldiers will come," Nthato shouted over the din.

David grimaced. "Yes, probably."

The throng marched on, a gyrating musical mass, swelling as students joined from Naledi and Molapo. David saw the first police, a small group cradling guns, outside Molapo Junior School. In front of Orlando West High School more police arrived in vans and armored trucks. They hastened into line, leading bristling German shepherds that blocked the road. David was near the front and didn't know it, but over three thousand students had massed behind him. A police lieutenant stepped in front of the dogs and in a strong Afrikaner accent said, "This is an illegal gathering!"

The students at the front laughed and jeered at him. He glared and said again, "This is an illegal gathering! Go home! Return to your schools!"

Someone grabbed David by the arm. "Time for you to go," Stephen said, looming over him. "This could be trouble." David nodded and moved back into the crowd. The students taunted the police, particularly the black officers, with cries of "Black power!" They sang freedom songs and chanted bawdy schoolyard rhymes, even as more and more police trucks and riot squads, unseen by the students, flocked behind the column of officers in front.

David didn't see who threw the first stone. Suddenly the students scattered, sprinting to the side of the road to pick up rocks. Faint popping sounds rang out. Some students, who had rocks, hurled them at the police, but as more shots cracked through the dry air, and it became clear that the police were firing directly into the crowd, the students began to run. David could smell the metallic smoke. He leapt over a muddy ditch and ran behind Orlando High. The shots came faster. A police dog broke free and ran into the center of the crowd, barking and snapping at the heels of fleeing students. A large high school boy kicked the dog in the ribs and it howled in pain, then turned on the boy and tore at his leg.

The gunfire ceased. Most of the students fled to safety, but many were staggering in the street, wounded by bullets or police clubs, and some stood wailing over fallen bodies. The police returned to their vehicles and abruptly left.

David wandered into the street in front of the school. Right away he could see it was bad. At his feet was a boy, probably ten years old, like him. He didn't recognize him. Blood had flowed from a bullet wound in his chest, but already the flow had thickened and stopped, and he was dead. David bypassed him and looked for Stephen. People gathered around the wounded and the dead. David rushed from group to group, asking for his brother, fearing the worst. But there was Stephen, organizing the panicky students, instructing them to carry the wounded to the clinic at Phefeni.

"Stephen, what happened?" David wailed.

Stephen's hands and shirt were smeared with blood. He hurried to another fallen body. David followed.

"Stephen! It was just a protest!"

"That's enough," Stephen said. "People are hurt. Help me or get out of the way."

David helped his brother carry the wounded to the clinic. They walked home afterwards, sneaking through alleys and backyards as enraged students looted and torched government cars and buildings. Riot trucks swept through the area, arresting anyone they got their hands on. Stephen and David hid every time a truck passed. David continued to sputter in anger and frustration.

"Let me tell you something, David," Stephen finally said. "This is just the beginning. First the police come to arrest people at night in their homes. Now they shoot at us in the streets. Soweto is going up in flames. Next is Alexandra, then the rest of it. Watch your ass from now on."

David nodded.

"They hate us and they're terrified of us. They're terrified of our faces, our numbers, the way we look, and our ideas. They arrested Mandela. They arrested Sisulu. They banned Steve Biko. Now they shoot us in broad daylight, and they don't care what we say or what the foreign newspapers say."

David shook his head. They left the fires and fighting behind and walked down dark streets, past shanties lit by paraffin lamps. David hurried to keep pace with his brother's long stride. "My school is burning, my friends are bleeding. Yours, too. People died today. We'll probably never know how many." He paused in front of the remains of a shanty hut, burnt earlier that day. "I know you're only ten years old, David, but your days as a child are over."

Stephen wiped a finger across the sooty tin. It was still warm.

"Over. Just like that . . ."

1

The drought had lasted as long as Bornwell could remember, and even the Olifants River had been reduced to little more than a silty trough spilling across the red rocks of the low veld. Bornwell spent one or two days each week attending to the boreholes, artificial ponds that sustained the wildlife of the Umhlaba Lodge region. It was difficult work. The valves of the pump houses were old and hard to turn, and many of them were labeled incorrectly, so, after investing great effort, he often found that he was draining rather than filling. There was no shelter from the sun at the boreholes, and in the middle of the day the temperature rose above 120 degrees. It was work the veteran rangers avoided, so it was left for Bornwell, a trainee.

Bornwell enjoyed working at the boreholes. As an apprentice, he was always being instructed and evaluated, and he accepted this. All the same, it was nice to be alone sometimes. He usually headed to the boreholes in the early afternoon and returned after sunset. The drive back to the lodge was the time he liked best, when the evening breezes dissipated the heat and the stars quivered to life above the Lebombo Mountains. On these drives, his spotlight sometimes picked out the twisted horns of a giant kudu or one of the elusive leopards that lived in the riverine bush near the lodge. If no further duties awaited him, he would linger outside the gate, his hands dry and raw from the wind that turned frigid as soon as night came, until hunger or drowsiness hastened his return.

Even out here in the bush, Bornwell knew change was coming. People had been talking about it even before Mandela had been released. He hoped the changes would mean a better life for his people in the cities and towns, as long as nothing changed in the bush. He wasn't naïve; he knew Africa had her problems, knew he was fortunate to live far away from them, in a wilderness paradise. He was lucky — and he knew that meant he had a lot to lose.

2

Alex Stanzis got lost all the time, even at home in Miami. His sense of direction was abysmal, he never paid attention to landmarks, and he refused to ask for directions. So he got lost.

When South Africa began emerging as a viable market in the early 1990s, Alex arranged an extended sales trip to exploit the burgeoning demand for the latest business software. Economic sanctions had made many of the most popular programs and operating systems hard to come by, but with the sanctions recently lifted, Alex wanted to be among the first software salesmen to visit this promising new territory.

After three years of intermittent planning, he finally went, but the trip was a disaster. As it happened, almost all of the companies he visited had already acquired the major software through the black market. He didn't even come close to covering the cost of his trip. It was the first time he had failed so completely, and the first time is always the worst, when the veil of invincibility is shattered beyond repair. He was only thirty-three, but he saw a vision of his future, replete with more catastrophes, and abruptly he felt old. He was angry, he was confused, and he wanted to go home. He would have canceled the short safari he'd booked had he not paid for it in advance. He had reservations for a four-night stay at Umhlaba Lodge, an exclusive safari preserve in the wilds of the Eastern Transvaal, bordering the Kruger National Park. He expected it to be well worth the $400 a night it cost him.

As he drove across the eastern landscape, twisting through rolling banana plantations framed by distant mineral mines, he dwelt on his recent disastrous sales presentations, remembering the surprise on the faces of the executives who, one after another, told him, "We're already using that application. Have been for months." He did all he could from that point on, and only his diligence and resourcefulness kept the trip from being even worse. He made a few sales, but it was still bad.

Umhlaba Lodge had faxed an excellent map to his Johannesburg hotel. Had they not, Alex certainly would have become lost, preoccupied as he was during the five-hour drive. He found the final dirt-road turnoff to the lodge and bumped along the rocky path for an hour. Boulders, rocks, and great clumps of weeds lined the road, obscuring his view of the bush veld beyond. He passed through the fenced gate of the preserve, but once inside, the only animal he saw was a single slim impala standing in the shade of a sausage tree. He arrived at the lodge at four o'clock. It was mid-March; summer was waning in most of South Africa, but the Umhlaba afternoon was grievously hot and dry. Johannesburg, with its 6,000-foot elevation and mild climate, offered no preparation for the heat that lashed into him as soon as he stepped from his car. A tall, thin young man with the darkest skin Alex had ever seen greeted him.

"Good afternoon, sir, and welcome to Umhlaba Lodge. My name is Bornwell Malaba. You must be Mr. Stanzis?"

"Call me Alex. Holy freakin' cats, it's hot! Is it always this hot?"

"Yes, I suppose so. It's still summer. Don't worry, it cools down at night. Please leave your bags, I'll have them picked up."

Bornwell walked Alex to his rondavel, a round, thatch-roofed hut, and left him there. Alex found the vents of the rondavel's air conditioner pointed straight up at the ceiling. He fiddled unsuccessfully with the vents before napping for an hour, after which he walked outside to have a look at the camp.

By five o'clock the heat had subsided ever so slightly. The camp, a cluster of a dozen rondavels and the large A-frame main hall, hunkered under a canopy of acacia and camelthorn trees. The ground under Alex's boots, hard, sandy basalt, had recently been raked. Footpaths lined with smooth river rocks curved through the flat, shady grounds. He saw only two other people, an older couple lounging alongside a small swimming pool. Bornwell walked past, and Alex called to him.

"There's something wrong with my air conditioner. It blows the air straight up. I need it to blow down, where I am."

"Yes sir, I'll have it fixed."

"Where is everyone? This place is deserted."

"Most of the guests are on a game drive."

"Any women here?" Alex said.

"Yes, some women."

"That's something, at least." Alex pulled a cigarette from his shirt pocket and lit it. "So what are you, the bellboy here?"

Bornwell laughed. "No sir, I'm an apprentice ranger. In one more year I'll be a fully qualified ranger."

Alex looked him up and down. "How old are you?"

"Twenty-five."

"Wow, you look like a kid — no offense. How long have you been here?"

Before Bornwell could answer, Alex saw what looked like a large, ungainly pig with a horse's head moving through the dense scrub at the edge of camp. "What the hell is that, a warthog?"

"Yes sir, you'll see a lot of them. They come into camp every day. Hyenas, too, sometimes, at night. Once or twice a month, there's an elephant that comes right up to the rondavels."

"Don't you have fences to keep them out?"

"No sir, no fences. We're all-natural here."

"What about lions? Don't they come into camp and, you know, eat people?"

"No sir, I've seen lions near camp, and there's a leopard who lives close, by the river. But we have a few Rhodesian ridgebacks—big dogs—that the lions and leopards fear. The dogs take care of the camp."

Four open-topped Land Rovers emerged from the bush as Bornwell spoke. They churned into the center of camp, bringing with them an immense cloak of dust. Their camera-toting occupants spilled out and trailed away in twos and threes toward the rondavels. Alex scanned the group before it dispersed. He counted twenty-five guests beside himself and the old couple at the pool. Most were older couples, severely overdressed in khaki, but he quickly noticed two young women who appeared to be traveling together.

The two girls walked from the Rover to a bench, where they sat in animated discussion. "Excuse me there, uh, Bornwell. Gotta run. You'll have the AC fixed, right?"

"Yes sir."

"Thanks," he said, without looking back. He walked to where the girls sat. "You just came from a game drive? How was it?"

"It was excellent," one said with an English accent.

"We saw the Big Five, all in the first hour," said her friend.

"Ah, let me guess—Scousers!" Alex said.

"That's right! How did you recognize the accent?"

"I lived in England for six months after college. I was in London for a few weeks, but then I was in Liverpool the rest of the time."

"Why Liverpool? Most people do anything they can to avoid it."

"Ah, I met a woman in London, she was from Liverpool, so we went back there."

The young women introduced themselves: Anna and Teri. They worked together at a hospital in Liverpool, Anna as a senior administrator ("I write memos all day") and Teri as a head nurse. After the three made plans to meet for dinner, the girls returned to their rondavel to wash off the icing of dust they'd acquired during the drive. Alex sat alone on the bench, forcibly attempting to acclimate to the heat. The empty Land Rovers ticked and cooled in the shade. The setting sun streamed through the trees and scattered its dappled light across the beaten vehicles. At the tree line, above the manicured grass and raked earth, the dry bush stirred with the measured breezes of evening, and, well past the trees, the heaving brown land hummed with the beating hooves and ragged claws of the wild things that lived beyond.

3

The guests took dinner in the boma, a round, reed-walled enclosure the size of a tennis court, open to the sky. The tables were arranged in a ring along the inside of the wall. An intimidating bonfire popped and groaned from the middle, providing light and much-needed warmth. The dramatic temperature drop following sunset took Alex unawares, and he shivered through his appetizer before caving in and fetching his jacket. The elderly couple from the pool sat to his right, Anna and Teri to his left, describing their game drive.

"We saw dozens of giraffes, too. Giraffe—giraffes—is the plural 'giraffe' or 'giraffes'?" Anna said.

"It's 'giraffes,' with an 's,' isn't it?" Teri said.

"Anyway—did you know, Alex, that lions sleep up to twenty hours a day?"

"She's an expert now," Teri said.

"And that giraffessssssss sleep for just a few minutes a day?"

"I didn't know that. I can't wait to get out there myself," he said, forcing enthusiasm he didn't really feel.

Alex thought Anna and Teri were both attractive, but not so pretty as to be disarming or intimidating. They were both short—Anna particularly so—and wore their hair in the current English women's fashion, that is, indistinguishable from the current English men's fashion. Neither seemed as remotely body-conscious as the women Alex knew in Miami, and he found it refreshing. No cosmetic surgery, no eating disorders, no colored contact lenses. He thought they would be fun to hang out with.

After they finished eating, the head ranger, a man with the physique of a rugby player with a third-grader strapped to his chest, dragged a chair next to the fire and took a seat. He introduced himself as Franz van der Veen and welcomed the newcomers—eight other people besides Alex had arrived that day.

"For you newcomers, let me explain a few things," Franz said. "First of all, as you know, we have no fences here. Don't leave your rondavel once you've turned in for the night. Anything you think you need outside can wait until morning. And don't wander too far from the footpaths at any time. Most animals stay away from camp. Don't bother the ones that do come here, like the warthogs, impalas, and baboons. Especially the baboons—they can be dangerous. A thirty-pound baboon would give me a pretty good fight, and I'm bigger than any of you. Whatever you do, don't feed any of the animals. You'll be signing their death warrant if you do, because they'll start hanging around expecting food, pestering people and becoming aggressive. When that happens, we shoot them. We have no other choice."

Franz's soupy, guttural accent, the English of the Afrikaner, was vaguely similar to an Australian accent, but without the twang on vowel sounds. For Franz and other Afrikaners, English was a second language, learned only out of necessity and used as infrequently as possible.

"When we go on game drives, don't stick your arms out the sides. On walks, it's very important that you don't talk. It's for your own safety. If you have a question or need to get your ranger's attention, snap your fingers or whistle. Walk in a single file and do not fall behind. Your ranger will remind you of those and other rules when you go out. Sounds a little restrictive, I know, but this isn't a zoo, folks. You have to be careful out here. Any questions?"

Nobody had any. "Okay. Let's meet at the Landies in ten minutes. Tonight we'll go out for two or three hours. Wear a jacket and be generous with the mosquito repellent. For all the lions and snakes out here, malaria is by far the biggest threat."

Most of the group went directly to the Land Rovers. Alex went to his rondavel to get his camera and brush his teeth. On the table next to his bed was a brochure outlining some of the animals they were likely to see on game drives. He thumbed through it until a knock on his door startled him.

"Mr. Stanzis?"

"Yeah?"

"It's time to go, sir. The others are waiting."

"Franz said ten minutes. It hasn't even been five."

"It's been fifteen minutes, in any case."

"Really? Okay, hang on." He grabbed his camera and followed Bornwell to the Rovers. Two had already left. The remaining one idled roughly. There was one seat open for Alex. He cursed himself when he saw Anna and Teri had left in one of the other vehicles.

They bounced along a dirt road, leaving the bobbing lanterns of camp behind. Franz drove in the right-hand seat, with Bornwell marshaling a spotlight from the left. The young man leaned forward, flashing the beam across open patches of veld and into creases in thick bush. He smiled and leaned into the frigid air.

Bush time was never routine to Bornwell. He'd come a long way to be here, having made the improbable move from his childhood home of Izolo, an impoverished shanty-town in Soweto, to a career in the bush. It was Franz's policy to employ mostly local people, the majority of whom came from the villages and farms around Kruger Park. Bornwell's city-boy advantage was that he had learned English at a young age. The local teenagers worked at the lodge as dishwashers or garden boys. Bornwell was isolated from them by his relatively lofty standing. Conversely, the rangers treated him politely enough, but they never included him in their card games or drinking sessions, because they thought he was too young. That he neither drank nor cared for cards mattered little; he got lonely. He enjoyed fraternizing with the guests and learning about where they were from, but they were always leaving — often without finding time to say good-bye.

Trying as it was, this lack of companionship served as a boon to his career. He had little choice but to spend much of his free time studying. Beyond the obvious, such as animal and plant identification, tracking, and being a good shot in a pinch, a professional ranger must demonstrate good off-road driving skills, fluency in native languages such as Zulu, Tswana, Xhosa, and Shangaan, rudimentary first aid, and, perhaps most important, an ability to socialize comfortably with wealthy foreign guests.

Even if he excelled in all these areas, Bornwell knew only too well that there was no guarantee Franz would employ him as a full ranger when he completed his training. At present, Franz had all the rangers he needed. If there was no job for Bornwell — well then, he would have to go back to Izolo. Back to city life.

The Rover trundled across the dark veld for ten minutes before Bornwell tapped Franz on the shoulder. The big man braked to a stop, took the spotlight from Bornwell, and probed into the thicket of mopane scrub where the young man gestured. A pair of radiant green eyes appeared briefly, then receded into the dark. Because they reflected directly back to the spotlight, only Bornwell and Franz had seen the disembodied eyes.

"What do we have?" Franz said.

"It was bushbuck."

"Just one?"

"No, there were others behind the tortillas tree."

Franz handed back the light. Bornwell found the bushbucks briefly, giving the guests their first look until the shy animals disappeared into the dark. Franz coaxed the Rover's abused gearbox into first. He drove slowly into the night. Bornwell's light occasionally picked out fleeing impalas and warthogs, but over an hour had passed since they entered the bush, and they still hadn't seen anything dramatic. Franz knew wealthy tourists expected to see big game immediately, and usually the night drives afforded them the best opportunity. He called the other rangers on his two-way radio and spoke in Afrikaans: "Anybody have anything?"

"Ahoy, cuzzie. It's quiet tonight," Peter reported.

"How are your bunch holding up?"

"Oh, they don't seem too bothered. We saw a few hyena right off the top, so that seems to be holding them over."

"Well, we haven't seen anything, and my bunch are grousing a little," Franz said. "I've got the Yanks."

"Ya, I noticed that."

"What about you, Hennie? You out there?"

"Ya, Franz. I'm at Eltskopdam, and it's quiet here, too. This English fellow I've got says the England-Australia one-day test match is on M-Net at eleven tonight."

"Ya, we'll watch it, but don't come rushing in yet. Keep them out there until they get cold, so they'll want to come in even if we don't see much."

"I will. It's just one of those nights."

"That's all right for you, Hennie. You've got the good-looking English birds," Peter said.

"Ya, cuzzie, and now I'm going to drive them to the darkest place I can find! See you at ten or so."

Bornwell gamely continued to flash his spotlight about. They had nights like this every few weeks, when the bush seemed dormant. Perhaps the lions were hunting on the slopes of the Mbari Hills three miles to the east, and the hyenas had found a carcass on the other side of the Crocodile River. Or the darkness might simply have cloaked the animals, which even then were watching them as they drove past.

A drowsy wind sloughed through the ebony and sausage trees, masking the scuffling of vervet monkeys in the branches. Franz stopped the Rover at the crest of a modest hill. He turned off the engine and the lights.

"If you sit in one spot, sometimes the game will come to you," he whispered.

They sat in silence for five minutes. Bornwell thought he sensed something coming close — he would not have been able to say why or how, whether he heard or smelled or saw something; only that he thought something was moving near them. But just as he was about to turn on his light, one of the guests burst into a sneezing fit. He released half a dozen violent microbursts, then blustered, "Sorry, sorry." Franz and Bornwell looked at each other and laughed. "Bang goes that," Franz said in Zulu.

Bornwell was sorry the guests wouldn't be seeing any game, but he was more than happy to lean back and watch the stars as they shifted across the dome of sky. Out here, unfettered by city lights or smog, they shone with an absurdly incandescent glow. Satellites streamed overhead in crisscrossing patterns, three or four visible at once in orbital freefall. The young boys who worked in the kitchen had a Zulu word for them that meant "the shooting stars that move very fast and never burn out." The Southern Cross, barely distinguishable from its background of mottled stars, trailed slowly but perceptibly above the haggard, grasping tree line. Meteors flashed every few minutes, trailing white sparklers as they burned through the atmosphere. Behind all of this lay a thick band of the Milky Way, arching across the sky like a tapestry of diamond dust.

Twenty minutes passed. Bornwell rubbed his arms against the cool breeze. Franz looked at him and nodded, then interrupted the group reverie when he quietly said, "Well folks, nothing doing. We get nights like this now and then, but don't worry. We'll see plenty tomorrow."

It wasn't too soon for Alex. He'd been genuinely excited about seeing lions, but as the night wore on and it became apparent none were to be seen, he wanted to get back to the little bar for a beer and, he hoped, a chat with Anna and Teri. As they drove back to camp, he began daydreaming about how he might yet salvage his trip.

The little bar behind the boma was unremarkable, and yet it had a history, which Franz and his rangers endeavored to keep to themselves. It had originally been constructed between the main hall and the cluster of rondavels, but late-night drinkers (rangers among them) made too much noise. So the bar—merely a thatched, three-walled shack, more Polynesian than African in appearance, and very light—was moved by Bornwell and a few rangers to an open area behind the boma, and two dozen comfortable outdoor chairs were arranged before it. Here the drinkers could make as much noise as they cared, without disturbing the visitors. Also, removed as it was, its open side faced a marvelous spread of bush veld, including a bend of the Ndephini River. Guests could sit in snug chairs facing this wild expanse, watching spider monkeys and warthogs move through the nearby tree line.

Cape buffalo, elephant, leopard, lion, hyena, crocodile, a fantastic variety of poisonous snakes—including boomslang, spitting cobra, green mamba, and perhaps Africa's deadliest snake, the black mamba — all could be found at Umhlaba Lodge, all a more than casual threat to human life. And over the years, the worst had happened more than once.

The lodge opened in 1957, and in that first year, a black mamba that had nested underneath one of the rondavels bit a garden boy. A year later, another mamba bit two Zulu housekeepers. The boy survived, but the two housekeepers died. In those days the camp wasn't as immaculate as it later became. Sacks of flour and cornmeal near the kitchen and the employees' huts attracted rats and mice, and these in turn attracted snakes. When the camp added electricity and refrigeration in the mid-60s, the snakes ceased to be a problem. But nothing can keep out the mosquitoes. A boy of nine, the cook's son, died of malaria in 1975.

But bad as those incidents were, none of them involved guests. That had to wait until a moonwashed night in 1990. At one o'clock, only the bartender, two Englishmen in their forties, and a young Canadian woman were still at the bar, just recently moved to its new location. Evidently the three guests were terrifically drunk by the time they stumbled off to their rondavels. The woman — the only survivor — had vague recollections of a suggestion to detour down to the river, a product of something less than sound judgment.

As they approached the water, a mother hippo and her young calf emerged from the river to graze the short-grass floodplains that bordered it. The three guests somehow didn't see them, and walked directly between the hippos and their safe retreat to the water. Game rangers would tell you this is a very bad situation, borne out in this case by the mother hippo charging with stunning speed. She trampled the first man into putty and clamped down on the second with her enormous jaws, very nearly biting him in two. Both men were dead on the spot. The woman escaped only because the hippo chose to stomp on what was left of her victims.

The incident made a few local papers. Franz decided to erect a small fence by the river, but it quickly fell into disrepair, inadvertently twisted and mashed by elephants. It was replaced once, and when the same thing happened again, the project was abandoned.

Good story though he may have found it, it would not have deterred Alex from his current mission. He found Anna and Teri sitting at a table in the bar. The rangers had gathered in front of the television, watching the England-Australia cricket match.

"Not interested in the game?" Alex said, dropping into a chair next to the girls without waiting to be asked.

"Perish the thought. We came here to get away from all that. Besides, it's just a one-day," Teri said.

"What's a one-day?"

"It means they just play this once. Not like a five-day, which is a lot more significant."

"I never got into cricket when I lived in England. Or soccer, either."

"No, you'd prefer your dignified American sports, like American football?" Anna said. "Honestly, that gear they wear; it's a ridiculous game, isn't it? Remember the movie *Rollerball*? It isn't far off from that."

"All that gear, it's dead silly," Teri said. "Rugby players don't need it."

"Ah, come on. Rugby's a neat game, but there's no way they hit each other the way football players do. If I could just take you to Pro Player Stadium on a warm fall Sunday, to see my hometown Miami Dolphins against, oh, Buffalo. Then you'd see what it's all about."

"And if I could take you to Anfield on a bitterly cold February day, to stand on the Kop and sing 'You'll Never Walk Alone' with forty thousand people during the Liverpool-Everton derby, then you'd see what it's all about."

"That sounds like fun. Final score, zero–zero," Alex said.

"Hopeless," Anna said.

"I could do without the rioting, and the being stabbed, and the skinheads singing racist songs," Alex said.

"Oh pish, most of that is in the past," Teri said. "Anyway, it's just more public than in America. Are you saying there's no violence or racism in your jewel of a country? What was all that we saw in the news going on in Los Angeles?"

Alex smiled. "Sure, we've got our problems. I think I know what we need to fix things, too: a royal family!"

"Oh no," Teri groaned.

"Be careful," Anna warned.

"Yes, that's what we need. It works so well for you guys. We need our own obscenely wealthy, obscenely unattractive, completely useless figureheads to distract our citizens from the dull misery of their daily lives. Works for England, doesn't it?"

Teri measured Alex for a moment, decided he was joking, and smiled. "Could it be that you're actually just a little jealous?"

"Actually, yes. Jealous of your wonderful weather. Your internationally recognized cuisine. And of your musical contributions to the world, which consist mainly of 'My Old Man Was a Dustman.'"

The girls laughed. "Actually my dad used to sing that song every time we went for a drive," Anna said.

"That, and 'My Old Man Said Follow the Van,'" Teri said.

Alex laughed. "I've been unfair. Apologies all around. Truce?"

"Truce," Anna said. "Who needs a beer?"

Before anyone could answer, Bornwell emerged from the darkness and approached their table.

"Mr. Stanzis, can you please come with me to your rondavel?"

"Why?"

Bornwell looked at the women and hesitated. "I can tell you when we get there."

"Ah God, what now? Please, just tell me."

"Well, sir, it seems you brought some fruit—some oranges—with you when you came?"

"Yeah, so?"

"And, well, you left your window open, and it appears a baboon has come into your room, looking for the oranges, which he could smell, and he . . . messed things up."

"Messed things up? How badly?"

"If you come with me, I'll show you."

As they walked through the dark camp, Alex said, "How come there aren't bars on the windows to keep this from happening?"

"There is glass in the windows, but they must be closed."

"Great. I guess this has never happened before, has it?"

Bornwell smiled gamely. "I'm afraid you're the first." He reached the door, inhaled deeply, and flung it open. Alex took two steps inside and froze.

"Holy shit! Look at this goddamn place!"

His clothes had been pulled from his suitcase and strewn about the room. The sheets were torn from the bed, which was covered with dirt, and his camera case had been knocked off the table. Bits of orange peel, dirt, and grass were scattered everywhere. In the center of the room, the baboon, evidently displaying a flair for the dramatic, had deposited a great steaming pile of shit.

"Great. Great," Alex said. "Goddammit! I can't believe this fucking shit!"

"Sir, please! Other guests are sleeping."

"I'm sorry, but shit! Look at this place! Shit!" He stepped gingerly around his clothes, picking mud off his expensive shirts. He cradled his camera and found to his relief that it was unharmed.

"I want a new room," he growled.

"I'm afraid there are no other rooms available, but I have already sent for someone to clean up. It may take an hour or so," Bornwell said, looking around the room. "Or more."

Alex picked up a half-eaten orange and flung it out the open window. "I'll be at the bar."

He stalked back to the bar, too loudly cursing the anonymous baboon. He paused to calm himself before rejoining the girls, but with the cricket match now over, three or four rangers had moved in and were garroting them with attention, beers, and slyly casual tales of bravery, competing with laughing ferocity for a favorable look. The men were older than Alex; sunburnt, fit men with weathered faces that fractured into splinters of creases with every full-throated laugh. They lived outdoors, they ate red meat two or three times a day, they drank beer. They called each other *"oke"*[1] and "cuzzie" when they were charitable. They dressed alike — khaki, boots, too-short shorts, wide-brimmed hats, dust. Dust was part of the wardrobe. There was no escaping it. They were the dust, they were the bush. Just another animal in the bush.

Single women were rare commodities at Umhlaba Lodge, and the rangers wasted no time in appropriating Teri and Anna from Alex, just as hyenas steal kills from cheetahs. In the bush there was little time for subtlety.

Although there were four of them, they'd carried their own chairs to the girls' table, leaving Alex's empty. He started for it, then paused. From the empty bottles littering the bar in front of the TV, he knew they'd had a lot to drink, and he knew therefore that he'd be lucky to get in three words. He turned his back on the light and noise of the little bar and walked back through camp. He settled into a recliner by the pool and vainly endeavored to find something of interest in the stars. After a fitful half-hour he went back to his rondavel and found it restored to its former immaculate condition, and after a perfunctory slug from the complimentary bottle of scotch Bornwell had left on his night table, he fell asleep. He'd heard people talk about how their thoughts and fears kept them awake at night. He had never understood that.

----

[1] *Oke* — dude.

5

From his table next to the lone window in his cramped hut, Bornwell watched Alex walk to his rondavel. There were always people like this, he thought. People who come to the bush expecting miracles, hoping that here, among the magnificence of the rhinos, elephants, and lions, the rolling hills, quiet rivers, and star-wealthy skies, they might forget for a day or two the troubles accumulated over a lifetime. They were inevitably disappointed, no matter how many animals they saw. If Bornwell had learned one thing from these people, it was that the bush changes no one. People take away from the bush whatever they bring to it.

He saw Sara, one of the waitresses, walking from the restaurant. Her father was Bennedict Vilikasi, Umhlaba's only black ranger. "Hey kid," she said. She always called him that, even though they were close to the same age. He smiled and waved back, hoping she would walk over for a visit. But she just smiled, hugged herself against the descending nighttime chill, and walked into the darkness.

He sighed and returned to his book. From time to time, talk and laughter from the bar drifted to him, but more frequently it was the familiar hoot and cry of jackals and hyenas, and the hiss of his lantern, which accompanied his studies late into the night.

6

The stars were still high when Bornwell woke Alex and the other guests. Along the eastern horizon a faint violet frosting presaged the coming dawn. They gathered at the boma and drank coffee and hot tea while the camp boys attended to the evidently perpetual fire. Teri and Anna walked over to Alex. "Isn't this heaven?" Teri said, rubbing her hands together in the brisk air.

"I'm not a morning person," Alex grumbled.

"Three Rovers are going out now," Franz said. "The other three will go out in an hour, for those who want a little time to wake up. You can go in any Rover you want. I suggest you try to ride with a different ranger each time, because each of them has his own favorite spots for finding game."

"You guys want to go now or later?" Alex said.

"Let's go now."

Soon they were rolling out of camp with Hennie at the wheel and Sandros, his tracker, at his side. Alex and the girls sat in the rear bench seat.

Bornwell rode with Peter Tovey, one of the rangers who took particular interest in the young man's education. As soon as they left camp, he stopped the Rover and said, "You drive." They exchanged places awkwardly and Bornwell piloted the vehicle through the deep sand of a dry riverbed. Peter turned to the guests and said, "Young Bornwell here is still learning, so I want you to ask him every question that comes to mind."

"I have one," a middle-aged Australian man said. "Yesterday, when we were out, I saw an old pile of bricks and half a chimney covered with vines and weeds. Were there houses way out here once?"

"This has not always been a wildlife reserve," Bornwell said. "Much of it was private farmland. There were Boer War battles right in this region. The land was bought and made into the preserve only forty years ago."

"What about leopards?" said an American woman. "We've been here three days and we still haven't seen a leopard. Are there any here?"

"Leopards are very hard to see. It's because of the way they hunt. The cheetah is fast, so he hunts in the open grasslands where he can run down his prey. So he's easy to see. The lion is strong and hunts in groups, so together they can bring down large animals, such as buffalo and zebra. But the leopard is not as fast as the cheetah, and, unlike the lion, he hunts alone. So he must surprise his prey. He hunts silently, without being seen. He lives in the riverine bush and ambushes his prey. So he's very quiet and hard to see. There are a half million leopards in Africa today, far more than lions. But for every leopard you see, you will see fifty lions. You can even find leopard tracks in fields just outside Johannesburg, but nobody ever sees them."

"I thought leopards lived in trees."

"No, but they often feed in trees, to be safe from hyenas and lions. Leopards can climb trees with an adult impala in their jaws. It's quite a sight. Sometimes they sleep in trees, but really they don't spend much time up there."

"Is it true that baboons are their favorite prey?"

"Not at all. Leopards are smart. They do nothing that

puts them in danger. Baboons have large, sharp teeth, and they are very strong fighters. A leopard will take a baboon sometimes, but it is much safer for them to hunt young impalas and warthogs."

After a few hours of driving they parked in the mottled shade of a giant baobab tree and snacked on sausage and cheese. While they ate, four enormous elephants walked from the heavy bush and crossed less than fifty feet in front of them. The guests scrambled for their cameras. Ten minutes later, when they were again on their way, they found seven spotted hyenas ravaging the tattered, two-day-old carcass of a buffalo that had been killed by lions.

Bornwell answered more questions as they trundled from the basalt pans to the riverine bush along a spruit, a small stream. By nine a.m. it was already above 100 degrees, and when the Rover passed from the sunblasted pans to the shady canopy, the guests sighed with relief in unison. This tiny vibrant refuge differed so greatly from the surrounding arid veld that it could have been a piece of a jungle tributary in South America. Umhlaba Lodge game moved warily through these leafy groves on their way to drink from the spruit. Despite the invigorating coolness, the ·animals avoided lingering here, for they knew that leopards lurked in the heavy cover, and lions waited across the stream. It was a permanent home to hordes of insects, and birds flitted from limb to limb in the green canopy.

"Are there many snakes here?" said Mrs. Maran, the American woman.

"Like this one, you mean?" Bornwell said. He pointed into the branches above them, where a green mamba slowly wound through the leaves. "It's a green mamba. He's poisonous, but very passive and usually stays in the trees. He won't bother us. He's not nearly as dangerous as the black mamba."

"I did my training at a lodge in the Manyeleti Game Reserve, north of here," Peter said. "One of the rangers was out with his tracker, doing a little road maintenance. They were hacking through an overgrown part of the road, when a black mamba reared up from the weeds and struck the ranger on the shoulder. His tracker lunged and chopped it in half with his machete, then retrieved the antivenom from a small ice chest in their Rover. It was kind of a fluke that they had antivenom. Most of us were pretty casual about it, and as often as not we left it behind. It has to be kept cold, which is inconvenient out here. Anyway, it was in a little glass vial, and as he carried it to the ranger, he tripped on a rock and dropped it. It broke on the rocks, and the antivenom was gone.

"The ranger sat under a tree and said, 'Put on a pot of coffee. I want one more good cup of coffee.' He was a real old Dutchman, he was happy to die in the bush. The tracker built a little fire and brewed some coffee. The ranger had his cup, then died."

"That's awful!" Mrs. Maran said.

"These days it might have turned out differently," Bornwell said. "The antivenom doesn't always work anyway. What we would do now if there was no antivenom is give artificial respiration. If you can keep the victim breathing, there is a chance he'll recover."

"Snakes are disgusting. I know it's a cliché, but I hate them," Mrs. Maran said.

"We need them here," Bornwell said. "They keep the rodent population in check."

"I know all that, but I still hate them."

"I understand. Don't worry. I'll keep us away from the snakes."

"Well done," Peter whispered in Zulu. "If these bastards knew how many snakes were out here, they'd be on the next plane home."

Before they started back for camp, Bornwell and Peter exchanged seats again. The Aussie who'd asked about the old farm remnants said, "Why'd you two change seats?"

"Technically, I'm supposed to do the driving," Peter said.

"I guess all that will change after Mr. Mandela is president though, eh?" the man said, and laughed.

Peter and Bornwell looked at each other. Bornwell turned to the man and said, "Peter drives because he is a fully qualified ranger. I'm still an apprentice. That will change when I pass my final examinations."

"Of course, lads. I was just having you on," the Aussie said.

Bornwell and Peter exchanged nods. The drive back to camp was quiet.

August 1983

After three weeks David Themba had memorized the extensive London Underground system, and every afternoon he let the subway carry him to a different part of the city. He soon tired of the museums and cathedrals, as teenage boys will, and began spending his time in the parks and gardens along the Thames. On a bench facing the gray water he worked on his school papers, taking relieved pleasure on the infrequent occasions when the sun broke through the clouds and warmed his skin. He filled page after page of his notebooks with his frantic scribblings. When the time came to transcribe his work with a typewriter, he found to his dismay that he was unable to decipher some of his own excited handwriting. Those original, inspired thoughts were lost, but, by the end of the term, no other student at the experimental high school had turned in such a great and mystifying volume of work.

On the last day of classes he waited with the other international students—Europeans, all of whom had remained strangers to him—in a well-lit and brightly polished hallway outside the headmaster's office. David was the first called. He took a seat opposite Mr. Henley, a short, balding, but strongly built man who incessantly cleared his throat.

"David, tell me, how have you enjoyed your semester?" said Mr. Henley.

"It's been fine. The accommodations here are much better than at home."

"That's a fine thing, but how would you characterize the learning experience?"

David shrugged. "It's been good. I liked that the instructors gave me the freedom to study my chosen subjects."

Mr. Henley leaned back and crossed his arms. "But you haven't been very happy here, generally. As we discussed last month—did it get any better?" As he spoke, he leaned across his desk and snapped open the blinds of his window, revealing a single tree branch that was pressed against the windowpane.

"I don't know. Not really."

Mr. Henley tapped his pencil on his desk and frowned. "I'm sorry about that. I thought you had a lot to contribute. I think it would have helped if you had tried to speak up more in class."

"It hasn't been all bad," David said. "I've learned so much. Not just from classes, but from living here. I've learned things so advanced that it will be years, probably, before I can make practical use of them back in South Africa." He smiled and stared out the window. "And my English is now almost perfect."

Mr. Henley opened his top desk drawer and pulled out a manila envelope filled with reams of paper. "You've done some impressive writing. I can't recall such a prolific student. But I'm still concerned with the confrontational nature of your writing."

"What do you mean?"

"Well, for a boy your age, to write with such hostility, it seems unnatural. This paper you wrote describing the Soweto uprisings of 1976, which you witnessed—"

David stiffened. "I didn't *witness* them. I *participated*."

"Yes, of course. I admit it must have been a significant

32

event. But to write all this material—" he gestured at the papers—"about that one event, and almost nothing about other aspects of your life . . . It's disappointing to me. What we hope for here is a sharing of experience."

"This is the experience I most wanted to share."

Mr. Henley smiled. "I respect your idealism. But I think this is why, perhaps, you've been isolated here. You never let your guard down. You never spoke, and all you wrote about was oppression."

David nodded. "I guess. I'm not so old, so I guess I just wrote about my memories." He looked hard at Mr. Henley. "All I remember is oppression."

Mr. Henley nodded. "Well, to business. Your instructors and I have evaluated your work carefully. You will receive eighty-five percent credit, which will be applied to your high school at home."

"Thank you. Can I have my writings back now?"

"Errr, they're supposed to remain here, on file, in order for you to receive full credit."

"I'd rather have the writings, I think."

Mr. Henley sighed. "No need for ultimatums. There's a photocopy machine in the library. You can copy your writings and return the originals to me. Or keep the originals, I'll keep the copies."

"Thank you."

Mr. Henley rose. "I would have liked to have been your friend, David. So would a lot of other people here, that's all. I wish you'd let that happen."

David felt a brief flash of regret, but masked it and simply said, "Sorry."

7

"We'll take a short walk here," Hennie said. "I know it's the lions and elephants you came to see, but I want you to learn about the bush itself, and all the little things that happen out here." He shut off the Land Rover's engine. "When you get out on foot, you get a real feel of what life is like for African animals."

Already they'd seen lions and elephants at close range, and the guests had fired fusillades with their cameras. But like all Umhlaba Lodge rangers, Hennie didn't want merely to show his guests the trophy animals. He wanted them to learn.

Sandros walked ahead of the group with his rifle slung over his shoulder. They crossed an open pan. Alex felt the heat of the ground through the soles of his Timberlands. His wide-brimmed hat bore the brunt of the sun's rays, but he still felt as if it was beating him down. The vegetation spanning the pan was thin and limp, leaves cloaked with dust. After crossing the pan, they followed a faint trail through a tangle of immature trees that provided little shade. They walked in a single file, trailed by a rising swirl of white dust. Alex looked behind him and saw the powdery curtain slowly sink back to the ground through the miasma of brown branches and vines.

"How long has it been since it rained here?" he asked.

"We're in a bit of a drought at the moment," Hennie said. "We get a little drizzle now and then, but it's been four or five years since we had a decent rainy season."

The line wandered through a stand of large trees and gathered around a depression several feet in diameter.

"This is a rhino midden," Hennie explained. "It's sort of a communal toilet for rhinos. They come here, do their business, and dig these little depressions. This one's been used recently." He kicked at the grassy droppings, uncovering a mass of glossy black dung beetles. "Watch how the beetles roll the dung into balls with their hind legs."

"Shitty job," Alex said.

"Ya, seems like it, but what other life do they know? This is the kind of thing I was hoping to see. These fellows are as important to the health of the bush veld as anything else out here. They bury and disperse dung before it can become a breeding ground for biting flies and parasites. Biting fly epidemics are serious. In some years, they've been responsible for the death of lions, who are vulnerable to skin afflictions.

"Also, the buried dung acts as fertilizer, which helps the vegetation, especially when we're in a drought. It helps keep the bush in balance. If there's adequate vegetation, the browsers and grazers have a good food supply. And if they're well-supplied, the predators will be, too."

Alex watched a single beetle roll a small ball of dung with his hook-shaped rear legs. It kept flipping over onto its hard shell back, its tiny legs pawing frantically at the sky. Somehow it always managed to right itself, and after a few minutes it disappeared with its booty into a thorny shrub. It seemed a painfully methodical procedure, given the enormous volume of dung.

"But how can they deal with all this?" Alex said, gesturing at the dung.

"Well, in a midden this size, there could be as many as thirty thousand beetles working away, under an inch or two of dung. They'll get it done. So while you might not impress your neighbors with pictures of dung beetles, they're a damn sight more important than they look."

They walked on for an hour. The only game they saw was a pair of giraffes that loped away at their approach. Teri and Anna kept pace with Hennie and Sandros. Alex, walking at the rear of the line, was held up by two older German men, who stopped every few minutes to scrutinize imagined animal tracks in the hard ground. Hennie admonished them gently a couple of times. He knew they'd caught the bush bug, and he respected that, but he didn't care to have them run down by a Cape buffalo on his watch.

By this time the day had become dangerously hot. Hennie watched his guests for signs of heat exhaustion as they trod gamely along the trail. As they passed through twisted valleys of scrubby growth, they occasionally found gaps in the vegetation, which opened onto vistas of the bush veld rolling in swells away from them. Little spruits and dry riverbeds meandered across the scarred brown earth like veins in an autumn leaf. The sky, a peerless blue, held no clouds, and the dryness of the air was distinct and palpable.

When they got back to the Land Rover they were covered with dust up to their waists. Because he had brought up the rear, Alex had inhaled a great deal of this dust, and his throat burned. During the jostling drive back to camp he imagined how the first beer would feel against his lips, and he whimpered with anticipation. It wouldn't matter that it would turn lukewarm before he could finish it, however quickly he drank.

It's not that Alex wasn't capable of enjoying the bush; if the conditions were just right, he would. But people like him more often find their pleasures in absolutes, such as a simple beer, rather than in intrigue and splendor on a grand scale. He wished he'd thought of that before spending $400 a night.

8

"There was a ranger named Terry who used to work for me here," Franz said to the group after dinner. "He liked to go out in the bush alone with an old eight-millimeter movie camera and film everything he saw. Hennie does that these days, and so does Bornwell. One time Terry filmed a pair of lionesses attacking a young hippo, which nobody had ever filmed before. He especially liked to film crocs. He'd hide out with his camera in a blind on his days off, waiting for impala or waterbuck to approach the water to drink. He got some great footage. We still have some of it here, but our projector's on the fritz at the moment, so we can't watch it."

Franz paused and lit a cigarette. All the rangers smoked. Bornwell leaned back in his chair and looked at the sky. Low, mottled clouds, the color of lead, scudded overhead. A few stars blinked through and seemed of the purest and most intense brightness by contrast. The fire cracked and hissed. Franz dragged on his cigarette.

"Terry used to make a lot of jokes about how one day he was sure to get taken by a croc. I think he actually was terrified and fascinated by them at the same time. I didn't like him going out alone. Once I saw some of his film that showed a fourteen-footer coming out of the water after him. He only got away at the last second, by climbing up the tree he'd been hiding behind.

"One day a few summers ago, not long after this drought started, he went up to Kortmansdam, a lake twenty-five kilometers north of here. He knocked around for a few hours, filming a few hippos and a smallish croc in the water, before getting ready to leave. He was on the bank packing up his camera gear when a thirteen-foot flat dog exploded from the water, grabbed him around the legs, and pulled him into the lake."

Flat dogs. That's what the rangers called crocodiles. In his accented English, Franz pronounced it "flet dugs."

Bornwell had heard this story many times before — it was a staple of Franz's — but his attention was nonetheless focused on the big ranger. A man who'd once had the unpleasant and extremely dangerous job of culling excess elephants from Kruger Park, Franz had also survived a cobra bite and "five or six" bouts of malaria. He was a good storyteller because he'd earned it.

"What a flat dog does when he grabs an impala or something is drown it right away. Their teeth are made for grabbing, not really tearing or chewing. They're quite blunt, really. So they drown their prey and either swallow it whole, if it's small, or pull pieces off by clamping on and twisting around underwater — the death roll. But because of the drought, the water was only a couple of feet deep, and since the croc had Terry down around the knees, he was able to keep his head above water. The flatty threw him around like a rag doll, beating him senseless, and finally he couldn't fight back anymore. He went limp and waited for the flatty to kill him.

"But instead, the croc let him go for an instant, maybe to get a better grip or because he thought Terry was dead. Terry realized this was his last chance and he made a dash for the bank, getting there just ahead of the croc and scrambling into his Land Rover. He somehow managed to drive back to camp, even though he'd lost a lot of blood and was hovering in and out of shock."

Franz paused again, this time for no discernible reason. Some of the guests stirred uncomfortably. The fire spat and snapped and began to dwindle. Bornwell stood and fetched logs and arranged them around the small flames. Franz helped him poke them into place before continuing.

"We got him to a doctor in Nelspruit. I visited him there the next day. He was in great spirits, considering what he went through—laughing and telling the story over and over. His right leg was pretty badly mangled and he needed about a million stitches, but they figured he'd be back on his feet in a few weeks. I remember he told me, 'Franz, I looked death right in the eye, and I cheated it.' Poor chap. I knew right then he wasn't going to make it."

Franz stubbed out his cigarette and threw the butt into the fire. "Flat dogs have all sorts of viruses and bacteria on their teeth, from the rancid meat they eat. Terry developed an unstoppable infection, as I feared. He died after a few days, sick, feverish, and in terrible pain. He survived a fight with a huge crocodile only to be done in by a bacterial infection." He smiled at his audience. "That's bloody Africa for you."

9

After the guests left the boma, sobered by his crocodile story, Franz smoked another cigarette and watched the fire deteriorate. Hennie joined him, pulling his chair close to the fire. "What happened to the 'this time I mean it' resolution, boss?" Hennie said.

Franz looked at the cigarette in his hand. "Ya, I know. Soon. I've told Pollen not to buy any more for me. Once these are gone, that will be it."

"Pollen buys cigarettes every time he goes to town, whether you ask for them or not." Hennie poked at the fire. "Boss, do you have any more Demerol?"

"Ag, Hennie, I told you already: if you weren't feeling better by the weekend we're sending you to hospital to get it checked out. A man isn't sick to his stomach every day unless something's wrong."

Hennie continued to poke at the fire. He laughed, but tightly. "Life's not worth living if you're sick, you know? I'd have poverty, I'd have prison before this, if I had to live this way forever."

"I've felt the same way, the first time I was down with malaria. I could have put a gun to my head."

"But at least you knew what it was," Hennie said.

"That's why you've got to see a real doctor, to get it sorted out. It might just be an ulcer."

Hennie tossed his stick into the glowing coals. "Why do you suppose we still get sick? Why do we feel pain?" The fire was no longer giving off much heat, so he moved his chair a few feet closer. "I mean, pain is evolutionary, right? A warning system for early hominids: don't bite rocks, don't touch fire, cover your skin when it's cold. Well, we've learned all those lessons now, but we still have the pain. And the only times we feel pain now, it's when we can't do anything about it. There's nothing to be learned, it's just needless suffering."

"Even so, you aren't considering the time scale. Evolution is a long, long process. It'll be millions of years before the human nervous system evolves and makes most pain redundant."

"It's not just the pain response, either," Hennie said. "Look at our vestigial organs, our tailbones and appendix, our body hair, even the hair on our heads. It's outdated — last year's model. Still, we're stuck with it."

"Ya. Excess baggage."

"Listen to this, boss." Hennie took a small piece of paper from his pocket and read from it. "'I've nothing to say of the sun and world — I see only the torments of man.' I saw it in a book and wrote it down. What do you think it means?"

Franz started to light another cigarette, but he saw Hennie looking at it, so he put it back in his pocket. "Beats me. We give work to the local people. We keep the poachers out. That's all I know how to do."

Hennie nodded. They sat without talking for several minutes. They heard something moving in the dry bush behind the boma, and they both knew it was the same warthog that came into camp most nights. They waited to see if it would enter the boma, but it must have heard them, because it suddenly ran away into the night.

"I've got this awful thing I've got to do," Franz said. He looked at Hennie. "What we talked about a few weeks ago."

Hennie nodded. He stood and threw a small log onto the coals, but it was too late. The log sat heavily on the dormant embers and did not catch fire. "Are you still going to do it on a seniority basis?"

"Ya, so you don't have to worry. But I'll have to let at least two go—maybe three."

"I'm glad I don't have to make those decisions."

"Be very glad, cuzzie." Franz pulled out a cigarette again. "Meanwhile, you're going to hospital Monday. And I'm smoking this one to your health."

10

Bornwell didn't have much free time. There were always boreholes to be monitored, leaky roofs to be patched, Land Rovers to be washed, and various other odd jobs that occupied his time in between game drives and walks. And always there was studying.

But after accompanying Franz on a morning bush walk, he found he had the remainder of the day to spend as he pleased. He packed a lunch, put new batteries into his old eight-millimeter movie camera, and headed across the bush in one of the older Rovers. He passed a small herd of impala standing motionless in the shade of a cluster of marula trees, patiently waiting out the midday heat. He parked at the foot of a rocky hill and clambered up its side with his rucksack and a rifle.

Bornwell sat on the cool, wind-smoothed boulders two hundred feet above the sun-lashed bush veld. He opened his rucksack and took out a sandwich and a wedge of jerky, which he ate slowly. Sweat beaded on his forehead and rolled in great drops down his cheeks, pattering into the stone at his sides. There was little wind, and again, no clouds.

Two giraffes moved slowly through camelthorn scrub below him. He chewed his jerky and waited until they came closer, then pulled his movie camera from his ruck-sack and filmed them for a few minutes. He could hear their snorts over the metallic whirring of the camera, and by the dark tufts of hair atop their small horns he could see they were both female.

After the giraffes moved away, he stood and examined the hilltop. Dead trees, gnarled and brittle, lay strewn across the rocks, the work of feeding elephants. That would have made for some good filming, he thought. All those elephants standing way up here on this hill.

Of all the great animals of Africa, Bornwell believed the elephant was the only one that seemed to display genuine emotion. It didn't bother him that they were dangerous and irritable beasts, capable of overwhelming violence and destruction. One simply had to be careful. He was in a Rover once with Hennie when a breeding cow suddenly charged from 150 feet. Often he'd been mock-charged, when the elephant would trumpet angrily with flared ears before pulling up short. But this time the cow pinned back her ears and lurched directly at them. Hennie recognized the earnestness of her charge and sputtered away, just managing to outpace her. What was funny, Bornwell recalled, was the reaction of the tourists onboard. They acted like it had been a ride at the fair, exhilarating but perfectly safe.

On two occasions Bornwell had observed Umhlaba elephants engage in inexplicable behavior. At a borehole he found several large cows clustered around the carcass of a young elephant that had died that morning. One by one, the cows approached the fallen elephant and ran their supple trunks all over its body, taking particular care to caress its stubby tusks. When each cow had taken a turn, they filed away, leaving the carcass to the waiting vultures and hyenas. When Bornwell related this story to his boss, Franz

44

confirmed that he had seen the same thing, too. He had no explanation for it.

The second, and still stranger, incident took place at the foot of the very hill where Bornwell now sat. Some months before, he found two young bulls scuffling in the dust, tossing and kicking a large rock back and forth. Sometimes they flung it with their trunks; sometimes they kicked at it like skilled soccer players. Bornwell thought it was merely the playful antics of immature bulls, but on closer inspection he was startled to find that the rock they were kicking was actually an elephant's skull. For several weeks, these same two bulls continued to play with the skull, joined from time to time by other members of their family, until they finally tired of the macabre game.

Bornwell paced across the top of the hill for several minutes, then sat in the shade of a stunted camelthorn. He sat for a very long time, watching the sun edge across the oceanic blueness of the sky. Surely, he thought, there is no sky bluer than that in southern Africa, where the hue is so rich it loses the appearance of depth and becomes finite and one-dimensional, like a freshly painted ceiling. Bornwell reached a hand up to it and blocked the sun from his face.

The afternoon heat abated, and a breeze curled through the cool green mountains of Mozambique and swept across poor, hot Kruger Park to stir the collar of his shirt.

The elephants, he thought, had it easy. For them, life was always the same. Eat, sleep, move, mate. No burning flags for them, no street wars, no change. The bush doesn't change. How far away from Bornwell's wind-smoothed boulder were the troubles of Soweto, how distant the ravages of cholera and typhoid in Izolo's foul water, how far away the bloody political conflicts Bornwell barely understood. He knew his country was soon to change forever. His generation would be part of history, and he was glad for it. But his place was here.

The sun set. The eastern sky flamed pink and orange for twenty minutes, then darkened to a benign violet. He would have liked to watch the stars steal up from behind the Lebombo Mountains, but Franz didn't like his men to be out alone at night. He hiked to the Rover in the fading light and drove back to camp, where he politely declined an invitation from the rangers and took his dinner in a folding chair outside his hut. Fish eagles cried from the river as he ate. Above him the stars pulsed salvos of steely light across the cooling red mantle of Africa.

Let others make history. His place was here.

11

"**H**ow did you enjoy your stay, sir?" Bornwell asked Alex as he walked with him to his car.

"It was cool. I hoped we'd see more lions, though."

Bornwell smiled. It was what almost everyone said when they left. Often he longed to shout, "Well, it's not a zoo!" Instead he said, "We saw, I believe, three different prides this morning, didn't we?"

"Yeah, but they were pretty far away. I doubt my pictures will turn out good."

"But even so, you can tell people how you saw lions and elephants with your own eyes, even if the camera didn't see them so well."

"People want to see pictures." He got into his car. "What's it mean, anyway? Umhlaba?"

"It means 'world.'"

"World. Okay. Thanks."

"You're welcome. Drive safe."

Alex started the engine and drove briskly out of camp,

ignoring the twenty-kilometer-per-hour sign and raising a huge swirl of dust. Bornwell watched the dust settle to the brittle ground. Alex was one of the last guests to leave. The lodge was closing for two weeks, so the rangers could conduct a controlled burn to thin some of the overgrown sections of the preserve. It would be hard work keeping the small flames in check, with the bush so dry. Bornwell kicked at the hard ground. It really must rain soon, he thought.

12

Bornwell sat under a tree outside his hut, watching a secretary bird pick its way through a line of scrub. Secretaries are snake hunters, and this one was in hunting mode. But before the bird found its prey, one of the young kitchen staff boys came trotting over to the apprentice.

"Hello *umnumzana*,[1]" the boy said softly.

"Hello *inkosana*.[2] How are you these days?"

"I'm well. Today I helped with inventory." He smiled proudly. "Then I saw the boss, and he asked me to bring you to his office."

"Thanks, Mangethusie. Would you tell him I'm on my way?"

"Yes, Bornwell. Thank you." The little boy traced patterns in the sand with the big toe of his right foot.

"Go well, Mangethusie."

---

[1] *Umnumzana* — sir.

[2] *Inkosana* — little master; term of affection for young boys.

The boy smiled again and sprinted off across camp. Bornwell went inside his hut and put on a clean shirt, then walked to Franz's office. All the guests were gone now, and most of the rangers had left for home. Only a handful, those who were conducting the controlled burn the next day, remained in camp. He couldn't remember the last time the camp had been so quiet. He half-expected to find zebra drinking from the pool and buffalo eating the grass in front of the rondavels, but instead found only a large warthog rooting through a flower bed. Sara, the young waitress, stood watching it.

"I think he's cute," she said.

"It's a girl."

"He, she. My father thinks they're ugly. He says God made them out of spare parts."

Bornwell laughed. "That's what I like to say about wildebeest."

"Well, I think she's cute." She gently reached a hand toward the warthog. The little animal snorted in alarm and trotted away with her tail held straight up in the air.

"She raises her tail so that—"

"So that the little ones can see her and follow her. My father told me." She sighed. "It's all you fellows ever talk about."

Bornwell wasn't sure what to say. "Your father's very smart," he offered.

"Of course. But there's a whole world besides this one," she said, gesturing at the bush.

He nodded. "Well, I've got to go see the boss."

"See you, kid."

He reached Franz's office in the main building and knocked on the door. Franz called him in and motioned for him to sit. He was on the phone, nodding and listening rather than speaking. Franz seemed stricken and even drawn.

As always, Bornwell looked with interest at the three large posters behind Franz's desk. Rather than the usual pictures of African wildlife, or local scenery, or rugby heroes, Franz decorated his office with vintage rock posters from America. In elongated letters that looked like they

were made from molten wax, one announced, JEFFERSON
AIRPLANE, GRATEFUL DEAD, MOBY GRAPE — FRIDAY, JULY 17 AT
7 PM AT THE FILMORE. Another one read, COME WATCH THE
PRETTY LIGHTS! SYD BARRETT AND THE PINK FLOYD! ALSO —
THE MOVE, THE NICE, AND AMEN CORNER. The final one was
smaller and less distinct, but it was Bornwell's favorite: FOR
THE FIRST AND LAST TIME TOGETHER! it blared in absurdly col-
orful, drippy letters. THE ELECTRIC PRUNES! THE UNCALLED
FOR! THE EXOTICS! AND SAN FRAN'S OWN QUICKSILVER
MESSENGER SERVICE!

Franz ended his conversation and hung up the phone.
"Thanks for coming so quickly," he said. "Look, Bornwell,
I'm going to get right to it. The owners have told me I have
to get the operating budget down — much lower than what
we're at now. There's only one way I can do that — I've got
to let a few people go. The only fair way to do that is seniority, so that means the three that have to go are Don,
Frannie, and you."

It was too unexpected, and the shock was too great.
Bornwell tried to speak but could only say, in barely a
whisper, "What?"

Franz sighed. "I've got twelve rangers and only three
decent Land Rovers. The only other option the owners gave
me was to start running ten Rovers through the bush every
day, which you know we can't do, because we'd wreck the
place. I already told Fran and Don. And there might have
to be more." He smacked his clenched right fist against his
desktop and cursed in Afrikaans.

The incalculable number of hours Bornwell had spent
studying began to slowly reel in instant-replay style across
the posters above Franz's head. So it was all for nothing, he
thought.

"I have to go back home," he said flatly. Back to Izolo.

"You can stay on for the burn this week. That way I can
give you a labor bonus. I'm sick to death about this, son. I
promise I'll do everything I can to get you on with another
lodge. Sabi Sabi, Idube, any lodge could use someone like
you. I know all those boys personally, and I'll put in as
many calls as it takes."

Bornwell nodded. "Thank you." Despite his best efforts he couldn't stop large tears from spilling down his cheeks.

"Really, you'll get another job, no trouble. And you know this place has been getting too big. Too many guests, too many people romping through the bush. We have to get it back to what it used to be."

"Yes sir, that's true."

"This is a severance check for two months' pay, to tide you over." He handed Bornwell an envelope.

"Thank you." He dabbed his eyes with the sleeve of his shirt. "Excuse me, sir, I'm sorry. I know there's nothing you can do. I'll stay for the burn."

"That's fine, Bornwell. You go relax for a bit. Take one of the Rovers for a drive if you want. I'll see you at dinner."

"All right." He stood and walked to the door. Before leaving he said, "Sir, just one question. I've always wondered."

"Sure, go ahead."

"Those posters." He pointed. "I've always wondered about them. What do they mean?"

Franz laughed. "They were here when I got here. They're so funny-looking, I've never wanted to take them down. They're rock bands from a long time ago. Before you were born."

"Ah, I knew that. But I always thought they were yours."

Franz shook his head. "Rock music, couldn't care less. But you've got to admit, the colors look nice."

13

The sun was high when Alex left Umhlaba Lodge at three o'clock. He hoped to get to his hotel in Pretoria by eight. Franz had all but insisted he take a few days to explore the capital, and had even suggested a moderately priced golf resort. Alex rallied his confidence and vowed to scour the city for last-ditch sales opportunities.

He ran the air conditioner at its highest setting, and made good time by exceeding the speed limit by twenty kilometers per hour. A lingering sensation of dehydration plagued him, so he pulled over at a small roadside shack that had a battered COKE sign hanging out front. Inside he found a slumped old man with sallow eyes and canyon-like creases across the terrain of his kindly face. The shack was piled high with African masks, wood carvings, pipes, drums, and other curios.

"What do you have to drink?" Alex asked.

"I have . . ." He opened a large ice chest and stood back to let Alex choose from the sodas and fruit juices inside.

"How much?"

"Sodas are two rand. Juices two-fifty."

Alex bought a can of apple juice and drank it as he inspected the masks on the walls. They stared back at him with bulging eyes, carved patterns on their cheeks, and terrifying shocks of hair made from zebra tails. They were creepy, and for that reason, Alex decided they would make good souvenirs.

"Where do these masks come from?"

"I make them. Me and my family."

"What are they for?"

The man rose from his chair and walked over to Alex. Despite his aged and bent frame, he walked strongly. He took a mask from its peg on the wall and held it in front of Alex. "They are spirit masks. They scare evil spirits and keep them from your home." He pointed with an arthritic finger to the teeth in the mask. "From a zebra," he said.

"They look pretty evil themselves."

"Ha, they do, but they are friendly."

"How much are they?"

The old man didn't answer. Another car had pulled up in front of the store, a new and very fine Mercedes.

"The prices are on the back. Excuse me, sir."

The door clattered open, and a large white man with a red beard ablaze entered. He spread his arms wide, as if accepting the accolades of a cheering crowd, nodded at Alex, then roared, "Thabo! I suppose you've been expecting me!"

"Yes, yes, Old Dennis."

"Let's have at it, then!"

The old man reached under the counter and placed a chess set in front of the big man, then said to Alex, "I have many more masks if you want to see them."

"No thanks. But I'll have another apple juice for the road."

The big white man, Dennis, turned to look at Alex. "See, Thabo? I tell you and I tell you. These masks are a waste of time and space. He doesn't want them, nobody wants them!"

"I sold four of them yesterday," Thabo said.

Dennis barked. "Really! I don't believe you, man. Show me the receipts!" He began arranging the chess pieces. Alex wanted to leave, but Thabo hadn't yet given him his juice. Dennis looked at him and said, "Sir, you don't mind of course, so tell me: would you have one of these terrifying masks in your home?"

"I was thinking about it. It might make a good present. They're exotic."

"Exotic? Exotic is just a nice word for ugly! Don't ever tell a woman she's 'exotic.' They know what that really means."

Old, bent Thabo shook his head. "You start," he said, gesturing at the board. He still hadn't given Alex his juice.

Dennis looked at the board for a moment, then back at Alex. "Ag, I beat him at chess, you'd think he would listen to me. I'm just trying to help, old oke! Clear out the masks. You're no tribal man anyway, you're supposed to be a businessman!"

"Uh, could I get . . . I'm just waiting for—"

"So, a businessman can be an artist, too," Thabo said. "And since when do you beat me? Not the last few times we played."

The game began with both men making rapid moves, seemingly at random.

"Another fine sale! Two cans of juice," Dennis said triumphantly. He aggressively moved one of his bishops across the board. "Thabo, you'll soon be able to retire!"

Thabo remembered Alex. He rose and opened his cooler. "No apple juice. But I might have more in the back." He walked into the rear of the store.

"Ah, old Thabo," Dennis said. He laughed softly to himself and met Alex's eye. "Like children, really, these kaffirs. It's a wonder they can even dress themselves."

"Who?" Alex said.

"Kaffirs, man. Blacks. And they think they're going to run this country soon. I'd get back to England if I was you."

"America," Alex said. "Then why do you play chess with him?"

"Ag, I like them just fine. But that doesn't mean they can run my country. Anyway, he's my only neighbor. This is my banana plantation." He pointed out the storefront, to the hilly groves of banana trees across the road.

Thabo returned with his juice. Alex paid the man and started to leave. Before he was out the door, Thabo had already captured Dennis's bishop.

"Better than you at chess though, aren't they?" Alex said.

May 1988

D ear Stephen,

Hey, my big brother. Problems, man. You wouldn't believe this fucking place. The first two months were good — Chris Hani was here, we had guns and food from Russia. They sent four North Vietnamese specialists to teach us how to make bombs, booby traps, how to fight a guerrilla war. We made two excursions back into South Africa. We were the ones who took out the South African Defense Forces radio station in Boksburg, if you heard about that. We had plans to hit a few more SADF targets, but then Joe Modise (he's chief of MK — ANC's armed wing) showed up. He kind of screwed everything up — Hani's been here for months, he trains and lives and sleeps with us in the bush. We trust him. Modise shows up, you can tell right away what kind of man he is — he gives orders, but he'll never get his hands dirty. He decided Hani was too popular, had too much influence over the men, so he sent him to a smaller camp.

After that, everything changed. No more training. All of a sudden, we're getting all these new men . . . but not volunteers. More like prisoners. Modise turned Quatro into a "reeducation" camp. He started with all the Marxist stuff right away. Anybody who resisted got beat up. The prisoners got tortured all the time. He's forgotten all about SADF, all about civilian Afrikaner targets. Whatever happened to "An eye for an eye, a tooth for a tooth?" Modise left after a few weeks, but his henchmen are running it his way now.

The whole thing is fucked. The ANC has sold out completely to the Russians. There's no way America and Britain will oppose apartheid and support the ANC once it becomes clear that the party is beholden to the Communists. This whole thing is a disaster, and I want out. I hope you won't say "I told you so," because I'm still glad I came. Before it went bad, I learned a lot of useful things here.

The abuses here—you wouldn't believe it. If you're reading this letter, then I'm okay. I trust the man I sent it out with. But if they found it, it would be over for me. Burn it after you've read it, seriously. There was a man last week, he'd been in MK for years, a loyal fighter. He disagreed with some trivial aspect of Marxist orthodoxy—I can't even remember, it was so small—they beat him in front of everybody to within an inch of his life.

I've asked to be sent back home; I've been here long enough now, so they said I could go back home for "insurgent activities." I should be able to slip away then, but I won't be able to come back to Kliptown. Somewhere else in Soweto, where nobody knows me.

I've been ill for a long time, too. Malaria, I thought at first, but it hasn't gotten better. I feel sick and weak all the time now. I don't know what's wrong. There were whores in camp last year, and I joined in with everybody else. Maybe the clap or something. I'll see a doctor when I get home.

I trust you are well.

Your brother,
David

Bornwell packed his clothes and books into three wooden crates he'd borrowed from the restaurant. He cleaned the little hut and sat down in his regular spot under a tree as the day slowly cooled. He always thought he would spend his entire life at Umhlaba. Only twenty-five years old, he was leaving for good.

He was concerned not only for himself. His mother depended on the money he sent home every month. Many times she had said he shouldn't send so much, but he knew better. She worked hard as a cleaning lady for a white family in Johannesburg. The Hartleys treated her well, but the pay was low. His father had died when Bornwell was a little boy, too young to have anything more than the vaguest memory of the man. He'd worked in the mines outside the city and died along with five other men when the shaft they were working in collapsed. Bornwell had two older sisters, both married and living in Kliptown. They had money troubles of their own. His cousin from his mother's side,

Chanda, a year younger than he, was no help to anyone. He had never held a job for more than two months.

Bornwell rose from his well-worn spot beneath the tree and walked through camp, saying solemn good-byes to the rangers and trackers who remained. He saw Bennedict Vilikasi, Sara's father, smoking a cigarette alone in a chair by the pool. Bornwell approached him timidly and said, "I guess you've heard?"

"Yes. I'm sorry to hear it."

"I just wanted to say good-bye."

Bennedict reached out a hand and they shook. "It takes a lot of luck to end up out here," he said. "Don't give up just because it didn't work out this time."

"I won't. Thanks."

"Sara wanted me to tell you good-bye. She said to call if you come back this way. Here's her number." He handed Bornwell a slip of paper.

"Thank you, sir. Go well."

"Stay well, Bornwell."

15

Alex woke in several distinct stages, stretched and rolled, and looked at the clock. "Shit!" he exclaimed. "Shitshitshitshitshit!" He'd forgotten to set the alarm. It was ten past ten, and his flight was scheduled to leave at eleven-thirty. He wasn't certain how long it would take to get to the airport, and he still had to return the rental car. "Cuttin' it close," he said as he stepped into a cold shower. At 10:25 he was out the front door with wet hair and a scribbled set of directions from the desk clerk.

He got lost almost immediately, turning left instead of right as he exited the hotel parking lot. The clerk had misunderstood, thinking Alex was parked out front, rather than in the side lot, and his directions were flawed accordingly. Alex soon realized something was wrong — the streets he was passing did not correspond to those listed in the directions. He decided to press on instead of stopping to ask for assistance. Already anxious because of his late start, he became flustered and angry. It is impossible to explain just how he ended up in Izolo—it involved several wrong turns. Even as he drove himself deeper between rows of listing tin shacks, he kept expecting to intersect a main highway. He turned around several times but couldn't remember how he'd ended up where he was. Soon he noticed that all the roads were dirt, and he could see only fragments of the Johannesburg skyline.

After three days spent exploring the jacaranda-lined streets of Pretoria, Alex was finally beginning to feel comfortable driving on the left side of the road. He'd even made it from Pretoria to his Johannesburg hotel without consulting a map. But this newfound confidence was no use to him now.

As he wound his way along a small, pocked road, he noted with mild unease that his was the only white face visible anywhere. He didn't yet realize he was in Soweto. He'd entered through one of the newer neighborhoods, and the transition from those relatively modern houses to the shanties, razed parks, and empty lots had been gradual.

Alex stopped in front of a rubble-strewn vacant lot, where two dozen scrawny kids raised a dust storm with a frenetic game of soccer. Two old men sat watching from a bench. Alex parked his car in front of a small store that appeared to be abandoned, and walked across the street to the lot. Approaching the old men cautiously, he asked if they knew how to get to the airport.

"Airport? Here?" one of the men said. He wore a tattered Boston Red Sox cap, a strange touch of familiarity that put Alex at ease.

"Yeah, Jan Smuts International Airport. I know I'm a little lost, but it can't be far."

"There is no airport here. But my name is Clinton, so . . ." said Red Sox Hat. He shrugged. "Clinton Larsen."

"Yeah, hi, I'm Alex. Well, I know there's not an airport here, but near here. Over that way?" he gestured vaguely. "It can't be more than fifteen minutes from here."

"Oh no. It's much farther," said Clinton Larsen.

"Like an hour," said his friend. "You'd need a car."

"This is Langdon Okpara," said Clinton.

"Hello, Langdon," Alex said, suppressing his exasperation. "I do have a car, fellas." He pointed to it. The two men turned and regarded it at great length — so great that Alex cleared his throat twice, trying to recapture their attention. The reason for their fascination entirely escaped him. His rental car was a nondescript hatchback, just like several others parked nearby.

The men turned back to him. "Now you've got a problem," Clinton said.

"Yeah, just let them have it," said Langdon. "It's what I'd do."

"Because you'll only get hurt," Clinton said.

"Since you are white," Langdon added.

"What are you talking about? Do what? Let who have what?"

At that moment, four teenagers stormed out of the dilapidated store Alex had parked in front of. They dove into his rental car without so much as a glance his way, started it, and tore away with dust streaming from the rear tires. Alex instinctively felt for his keys in his pocket and remembered he'd left them in the ignition.

"Son of a mother pus-bucket! What the fuck!? They stole it!" he spat, his arms flailing above his head like the tentacles of an octopus dropped from a tree.

"Yeah, they do it all the time," Clinton said.

"Okay," Alex said, trying to compose himself. "Screw the car, it's a rental. But goddammit, my wallet, my passport, my camera . . . shit." He paced in front of the men. They lost interest in him after a few moments and turned back to the soccer game.

"Good pass," Clinton commented.

"Yes, he's going to be a good player. He keeps his head up when he's dribbling and sees the whole field. Like Jomo Sono, when he was a boy, remember?"

"Can you be serious? You're comparing that flea to Jomo Sono?"

"Give him time, he'll develop," Langdon predicted.

"Hey, excuse me," Alex said. "I know you're busy with the World Cup there, but my car, remember? What about the police?"

Clinton shrugged. "You can go to them, but they won't be interested. Your car is probably being painted right now. They won't find it. They never do."

"Well, shit." He examined his surroundings. "Can you show me where the police station is? At least I can use a phone there."

"There's no police station here. They come from Johannesburg. But you can find a phone nearby. Try Kaiser's, a few blocks that way." Langdon pointed.

"Is it safe?" Alex couldn't help but notice a group of tough-looking teenagers staring at him from across the field.

"Safe enough. You've already lost your car and wallet, so you won't be any good to anybody." Langdon smiled. "Good luck, mister."

"Thanks." Alex started down the street in the direction Langdon had indicated. The men's voices still reached him.

"The kid's good, sure. What's his name?"

"Papi Khomane," Langdon said. "He's already training with Pirates."

"I'll remember that. He's good, but there's only one Jomo Sono."

16

Stranded on foot, with no money, no identification, and no idea where he was, Alex couldn't have been more conspicuous. Despite this, he felt neither threatened nor vulnerable.

He walked hurriedly past corner shops where men sat on curbs or leaned against walls of splintered wood. Rain from the previous night had turned the road into a glossy bed of red mud. Alex tried to protect his shoes by stepping lightly through the deeper patches, but he abandoned this as an extravagance of attention he could not afford. The storefronts gave way to more vacant lots. He crossed one, walked past a small, cavelike bar, and continued along a parallel street that seemed to hold more promise. It didn't occur to him to poke his head into the bar to look for help — he'd caught a peripheral glimpse of a group of tough-looking men standing in the doorway and hurried along. Had he gone inside, he would have been surprised indeed to find Bornwell Malaba, home again after his unfortunate departure from Umhlaba. He was enjoying a beer with his cousin Chanda.

Bornwell had seen Alex and had been only mildly surprised. The tourists were always doing and saying incomprehensible things. He pointed Alex out to Chanda. "Did you see that white fellow?" he said in Zulu. "He was at the lodge only last week."

Chanda laughed. "What's the bastard doing here?"

"Who knows?"

"Umhlaba guest, walking through Soweto," Chanda said. "We know he's rich. Why don't we roll him?" he joked.

"Right, I keep forgetting what a criminal mastermind you are. I bet he's looking for a whore," Bornwell said. "He spent most of his time chasing two English birds."

"How'd he make out?"

Bornwell shook his head. "Bombed." He swigged his beer. "Walking around here like this, he's a big strong guy, but imagine if the APF or Kusasa see him?"

"Aha," Chanda said. He smiled at Bornwell. "Kusasa."

"Oh no," Bornwell said.

"I'll take him to Kusasa. David will pay good money for a white foreigner. He English?"

"American. So you're in the kidnapping business now? Big step up from grocery clerk."

"I quit last week. They wanted me to keep showing up, day after day, at six in the morning. Imagine!"

"Outrageous," Bornwell said flatly, playing along.

"Anyway, think about it: we go to him, tell him we'll help him get his whore, or his drugs, whatever it is he wants, and we send him to David. He'll reward us well, and we need it. You don't have a job either."

"I know you aren't serious, anyway, but I do think I should probably try to get him out of here. If he gets himself into trouble, or hurt, it could reflect badly on Franz." He finished his beer. "Let's go find him, yeah?"

"Yeah, but I still like my idea better."

"We better hurry. This is the guy who had a baboon shit in his room. And he thought there were tigers in Africa."

Chanda thought so, too.

"What an idiot!" Chanda said. "Tigers in Africa!"

"I know."

They walked outside into the bright sun.

"Where *do* they live?"

"Tigers? India. A few in Siberia."

"What about the American woman you told me about once, she thought crocodiles were vegetarians?" Chanda said.

Bornwell laughed. "No, her husband asked me what was the difference between American alligators and Nile crocs. Before I answered, the woman said, 'These crocodiles are meat-eaters. Our alligators just eat plants.' And there was another American once who thought rhinos were poisonous."

"No. No, I'm not believing that one."

"I tell you! He thought their saliva was poisonous. Rich people are some of the stupidest people ever."

Chanda whistled incomplete tunes as they walked. Bornwell saw the way Chanda was thinking—he could see it clearly in his face when Chanda was scheming—and he became annoyed. "Don't make too big a deal out of this, Chanda. This guy's an idiot, and he's not very nice, and I just don't see much good coming out of it."

Chanda shrugged. "It's worth a try. How often does opportunity come to Soweto?"

A lex woke abruptly this time. It was still dark, and in his grogginess he couldn't make out his surroundings. His right shoulder and face were wet. He sat up and in the alley's dim gloom made out the time on his watch. It was four-thirty in the morning.

He'd stumbled across this sheltered alley shortly before midnight, exhausted, defeated, having found not assistance but rather hostility and laughter on the streets. In actuality, several people had been willing to help him, but he misinterpreted their initial amusement at his predicament, and their good intentions were wasted.

Once or twice he'd glimpsed a pair of shadowy figures trailing behind him, and he was sure he was being followed. But when he found the alley and the mass of flattened cardboard boxes, he gave in to the urge to sleep. He was pretty sure he'd given the two men the slip when he ducked into a doorway and watched them walk past.

He settled back onto the damp cardboard mat, but sleep

wouldn't come again. After an hour he rose and continued down the street that he thought might lead him to the edge of Soweto and the highway, where he might hitchhike or even walk to the airport. What he needed most was a phone. A few phone calls would sort it all out. He'd found a few pay phones since getting lost, but none of them had worked.

Early-morning fires burned. The smell of pots of beans and mealie-meal—a sort of porridge—bubbling away sent painful flashes of hunger through his gut. The last thing he'd had to eat was a doughnut, as he was rushing to leave the hotel the previous morning. After all the walking he'd done and after the fitful, damp sleep, he felt his body begin to systematically shut down. His step wavered, his vision blurred, and he coughed, his cough dry and ragged. Sweat beaded on his forehead and pooled under his eyes, despite the morning chill, and he plopped to the ground to rest. He sat cross-legged for a few moments before his eyes rolled back into his head and he toppled over, unconscious.

18

Chanda glared at his little brother Marks, who stood poking him in the shoulder. "Stop it," he said, rubbing a hand across his face. "Let me wake up, at least. What's the matter?"

"There's a white man outside," Marks said.

"So what?" He sat up.

"He's in the street, just close. He's sick I think. He's sleeping in the mud."

"Oh hell. Well, I'll go see."

"I'll go too," Marks said.

"No, fill a tub of water for me."

"What for?"

"For this man, and for me."

Chanda found Alex in the street. He was disappointed; he was hoping this man was the lost Umhlaba guest, but that couldn't be so. This man was covered in mud, dried to a crust in some places, fresh and wet in others. Perhaps his clothes were once clean and fashionable—and, true, Chanda detected no holes or tears in them—but they were too stained, wrinkled, and muddy to belong to a rich American tourist.

He tried to wake the man, but Alex only mumbled incoherently, so Chanda dragged him into the shanty. Marks brought him the water, and he splashed some on the man's face. This woke him; he sat up and grasped his head, then wiped the water and mud from his face. Chanda smiled down at him, then said something in Zulu to Marks and the other children who were crowding behind him. Alex managed a bleary smile and a wave and said, "Hi."

"Hello," Chanda said.

Alex looked around. He was inside somebody's home. It was small and clean, with sound wooden floors, but very dark—the windows were boarded over.

"I got lost," Alex said. "Jesus . . . car stolen, missed my flight. Jesus." He laughed.

"Were you at Umhlaba Lodge?" Chanda said.

"Yes! Shit! How'd you know?"

"You remember Bornwell from there? He's my cousin. We saw you yesterday and tried to help you, but you ran from us."

"Ah shit, that was you guys? Shit."

"If you stay here, I'll go get Bornwell."

"Okay. Wow. Thanks, man."

"I'm Chanda. That's Marks," he said, pointing at his brother. "The others are—well, Marks will tell you. I'll be right back." Then he turned to Marks and in Zulu said, "Marks, don't let him go outside, and don't let the others out, either, until I get back. I don't want anybody knowing he's here."

"But you pulled him in from the street in front of everybody. Look." Marks pointed out the front door, where a few neighbors were rubbernecking, trying to get a look at the white man.

"That doesn't matter; they'll get bored and go away if they don't see him again. Just stay put."

Chanda hurried over to Bornwell's house. He was glad for this new diversion. It would be something to do for a day or two, at least, and maybe the American would reward them for their help. It was bound to be better than looking for another job. He heard the same thing every time he applied—"no qualifications"—even though he had managed to graduate from high school, a surprise to everyone, especially himself, given his penchant for skipping class. In one memorable stretch, he skipped school for seventeen consecutive days, going off each morning dressed for school and carrying his books, then sneaking away to watch the Orlando Pirates soccer team in training. The school finally noticed his absences and sent a note to his mother. But Marks intercepted it, gave the note to Chanda, and told him he'd better consider going back to school. Chanda did, but his laziness simply found other outlets.

After graduating, he took and quit half a dozen jobs in one year. He began holding out for the "right" job. Chanda believed he was destined for greater things, and didn't want to be behind a counter or down a mineshaft when opportunity came knocking. He tried every get-rich-quick scheme he'd heard of (the least profitable being selling used refrigerators on the street. He ended up with six broken-down refrigerators in front of his mother's yard, after the sale of just two, for a five-day total of seven rand). Undaunted, he waited for the big break that was sure to come. Perhaps the American would be it.

"Bornwell! Get up, man!" Chanda drummed gently on Bornwell's window.

Bornwell was already awake. He pulled back his curtain.

"Open the window," Chanda said.

"It's cold."

"Open it, man! I've got news."

"Wait, I'll come outside."

Chanda sat on the front step. Bornwell came out and sat next to him. "What is it?"

"That American man, Alex."

"Yeah, forget him. I'm not going all over town looking for him today."

Chanda smiled. "He's at my house. "

Bornwell gaped. "Are you serious? How? Did you follow him all night?"

"No, it's the strangest thing. This morning he was sleeping in the street right out front! Marks found him there an hour ago. I pulled him inside and washed the mud off him. He was still asleep, really."

"What does he say?"

"He jabbered at first, then said something about getting lost and having his car stolen."

"Ha! Ah, now that's a bit funny. He was so arrogant, Chanda. You should have seen him in his expensive clothes."

"Not worth anything now, all covered in mud."

"What about your mother? What did she say about him?"

"She had already gone to work before Marks found him. I guess she didn't see him, or ignored him. Anyway, I told him I would go get you."

Bornwell sighed. "Yeah, fine. Let's go."

With the smokestacks of the distant mines framing the city, they walked the muddy lanes to Chanda's. As they got closer to his cousin's house, Bornwell was unaccountably filled with mild dread at the thought of seeing Alex Stanzis again. Perhaps it was because the American would be a painful reminder of his happy life at Umhlaba, only a few days removed but already seeming like ancient history. Or perhaps he recognized an uncomfortable parallel—he didn't belong here any more than Alex Stanzis did, but nobody was coming to save him.

19

Just a few blocks from Chanda's house, they saw a group of ten or so men standing in a weedy vacant lot. Chanda knew right away they were members of Kusasa, a gang of thugs. One of them, David Themba, called out to Chanda. Chanda waved back at him. "Oh shit. I'll meet you at my house," he said to Bornwell. "Go on ahead. Let me see what David wants."

Despite being a few years older, David had always been very friendly toward Chanda. David was Kusasa's founder and leader, and sometimes when he saw Chanda he encouraged him to join. In truth, Chanda found the idea morbidly attractive—it might be a way to make some money. But David was known as a thug, and in recent years had become more intense and unpredictable. Chanda was scared of him.

"Hey, man," Chanda said casually.

David nodded and they slapped palms. "Chanda, did you see the white man who was wandering around town yesterday?"

"Yeah, me and Bornwell were at Kaiser's and we saw him walk by, but we didn't think anything of it."

"Will you tell me first if you see him again?"

"Sure, man."

"Good. APF, if they find him, they'll just shoot him. They're too stupid to know better."

"Why do you want him?" Chanda ventured.

"Oh, I'm just curious. I wonder who he is and what he's doing here. Who knows, he might be important to someone."

David stepped close to Chanda so the others couldn't hear. "Have you seen Pirates play much this year?"

"No, just once. The tickets are too expensive."

"But your cousin Ekeke, he still plays for Pirates. He can't get you tickets?"

"He's my brother-in-law. My sister's husband. He only gets two each match, and he gives those to his wife and son."

David smiled. "I have some extras." He pulled three paper slips from his back pocket. "Three tickets to Saturday's match with Kaiser Chiefs. Go, man, have a good time."

"You better enjoy it," said one of David's friends, a small man with dreadlocks twisted into his beard.

Chanda was overwhelmed. Chiefs versus Pirates: the biggest match of the year.

"What, man! Thanks!"

"It's okay," David said. "But remember, brother, come to me if you see the white man, or if you hear any of the drunks at Kaiser's talking about it, okay?"

"You got it."

David put his arm around Chanda's shoulders and drew him away from the others. "Is your father still at Kimberley?"

"Yes. For another month, at least."

"He should find other work."

"That's all he's ever done," Chanda protested.

"Man, the mines are a death sentence." David shook his head.

"Okay, David, I'll tell him. Thanks, thanks. Go well."

"Stay well."

After Chanda was gone, one of the others said to David, "Why are you always so easy on him?"

"Because he's going to be a big help to me one day."

"Him? Why?"

"He's smart, and he's a coward. The rest of you, you'd run straight through fire if I told you to, but he looks out for his own ass first. If I don't get someone like him, there'll be nobody left after it happens." David lit a cigarette. "Besides, he's smart. You can tell by looking at him."

"Really? How?"

"He's fat. Everyone else is just about starving, but he's fat. He must know something we don't."

20

Chanda caught up with Bornwell just before reaching his house. "Hey, man, we've got a problem," Chanda said.

"Yeah?"

"Yeah. David wants this guy. He wants to kidnap him."

"He said that?"

"Not exactly," Chanda said. He wiped sweat from his forehead. "He said something like, 'He might be important to somebody.' What he means is he might be important enough to somebody that they'd pay money to get him back."

"Shit," Bornwell said. He looked around. "Do the neighbors know he's here?"

"Yeah, a couple of people saw him, but they're just old women. Nobody'll listen to them even if they say anything."

"Even so, we better get him out of here fast. Let's go talk to him."

They started inside, but Chanda stopped Bornwell. "I

forgot! Look what he gave me!" He showed the tickets to Bornwell.

"Holy wow. Shit! Why?"

"I told him I'd help him find the white man. Ha!"

Bornwell groaned. "That gives us two days to get him out of Soweto."

They went inside. Bornwell shook Alex until he woke.

"Bornwell! Ah dude, I'm glad to see you. Shit." Alex rubbed his face and smiled.

"How are you, sir?" Bornwell said. "I'm sorry for all your troubles."

"Well, it could've been worse. Your cousin here saved my ass."

"Mr. Stanzis, what are you doing here? What happened to you?"

Alex told his story. They struggled not to laugh when he told about his car being stolen, but Bornwell turned grim when Alex told him he'd lost his wallet, passport, and airline ticket.

"Bad stuff," Bornwell said.

"It shouldn't be a big deal," Alex said. "Just get me to a phone. Your lodge should have my credit card on file, right? I'll have to cancel it, but I should be able to get a replacement. Then I can buy some clothes and get a new ticket home."

"Yes, but we've got a bigger problem now. There are some dangerous people looking for you," Bornwell said.

"What people?"

"Ah, it's a group called Kusasa. They're a gang of thugs. They're supposed to be political, but basically they just steal and rob."

"They want to kidnap you," Chanda explained helpfully.

Alex looked at Bornwell. "Seriously?"

Bornwell nodded.

"Hm. Fuck."

"Actually, they are political," Chanda said. "David started it because he didn't like either of the main resistance parties, the ANC—African National Congress—and the IFP, the Inkatha Freedom Party. So he started Kusasa, because he wanted to make things better for township people, but other gangs started trouble with him right away, so he had to get some muscle, too."

"Who the hell is David?" Alex asked.

"David Themba is the Kusasa 'leader,'" Bornwell said. "Chanda's defending him because they're friends."

"We're not friends," Chanda said. "Bornwell doesn't know anything. He's been in the bush for too long. David's nice to me, but we aren't friends. I hardly ever even see him."

"Uh-huh, except he just gave Chanda three tickets to the biggest football game of the year."

Chanda looked angry. "Bornwell, again, doesn't know anything. To David, the tickets were nothing."

Bornwell laughed. "Why don't you tell Mr. Stanzis why David gave them to you?"

Chanda grinned sheepishly. Alex said, "Well?"

"Ah, well, he gave them to me because he wants me to tell him if I see you. I won't, of course."

"But you took the tickets," Bornwell noted.

"Get back to Kusasa," Alex said.

"Oh yeah, well, like I was saying, over the last couple of years, they've gotten pretty violent around here. David recruits new members because they keep fighting with the other gangs. David's a smart guy. He really did want to do good at first, but now he's caught up in these gang wars. They have about two hundred members now. He asks me to join every now and then, but I always say no thanks, and he never pressures me."

Alex nodded. "And you think he's serious about kidnapping me? He'd really follow through on something like that?"

"Definitely," Chanda said. "He carries a gun, they all do. Violence is nothing to them."

Alex stood and paced the small room. "I gotta get the fuck out of here."

"That's what we were thinking," Bornwell said.

"Only it won't be easy," Chanda said.

"And it could be dangerous for me and Chanda,"

Bornwell said. "I mean, even if we get you out, David could find out later that we helped you."

"Yeah, I hear you. You want me to make it worth your while."

Bornwell and Chanda looked at each other. "We weren't thinking about money," Bornwell said.

"But we did both just lose our jobs," Chanda pointed out.

Alex looked at Bornwell. "You got fired?"

"Not fired, exactly. Laid off. The lodge had more rangers already than they needed."

Alex nodded. "That's too bad. You were good, man. Shit. I had a good time there, I guess. I just wasn't in the right mood to enjoy it." He sighed. "Okay. I'll, uh, compensate you guys, but it will have to wait until I get a credit card."

"We'll take you to Johannesburg, but it won't be easy. Let me and Chanda think about it for a while."

"Cool. I could sleep some more, if that's okay."

"Go ahead. We'll wake you if we need you."

Chanda and Bornwell walked into the small backyard and sat on the hard ground. The day was bright and warm, but much cooler than the scorching low-veld days Bornwell was accustomed to. Despite the close proximity of other shanties, it was quiet. They watched an old woman fill a jug from the muddy ditch that ran between the shanties.

"A whole family of Germans walked right through here a few weeks ago, and nobody got excited about it. I wonder why it's different now?" Chanda said.

"I don't know. Probably because of the tension. All this violence between the ANC and IFP, all the talk about the election, change, revolution . . . It feels different from the last time I was here."

Chanda nodded. "So what do we do with him?" He jerked a thumb back toward the house.

"We can just put him on a minibus to Joburg. It'll cost just a few rand and be easy."

"No. The driver will take him straight to Kusasa or APF or someone else who'll pay more for him than a few rand for a ticket. It'd have to be a real taxi from Joburg, but they're expensive, and they don't come into this part of town anymore anyway."

"What if we had more money? I mean, if we had enough, we could hire someone to come right here to the front door, in the daytime, and take him right to the airport," Bornwell said.

"Well, sure. But how much money do you have? I'm broke."

"Oh no, you aren't. You've got a hundred rand right there in your back pocket."

Chanda leapt to his feet. "The tickets? No!"

"Yes, man. We sell the tickets, we use the money to hire a driver, and Alex pays us back. And then some."

Chanda frowned and sat back down. "Yes. But no, no. David will expect to see me at the match. If we don't show up, he might suspect something."

"Man, you should have just walked away when you saw him. We're trying to get this guy out of town, and you're taking presents from the guy trying to find him."

Chanda shook his head. "I only hope . . ."

"What?"

"I hope Marks Maponyane is fit for the match Saturday. He's had a bad knee all season. You know how much Pirates depend on him."

Bornwell groaned. "We've got way bigger problems to deal with. Shit. Fucking David Themba. I never thought I'd have to deal with him. Shit." He scraped up a small amount of mud with a finger and threw it at Chanda. "How bad is Maponyane's knee?"

21

Bornwell, Chanda, and Alex killed the day at Chanda's house. After sunset, they hurried to Bornwell's house, where Bornwell explained the situation to his mother. The woman was alarmed at first, but quickly succumbed to her son's gentle assurances. She smiled at Alex and said, "It's a shame this trouble you have. Try not to worry."

Bornwell said, "I'm going to go to a phone and call Franz. You remember Franz, the head ranger?" Alex nodded. "I'm sure when he hears of your trouble, he will want to help. He always helps visitors to his lodge."

"I'll go too," Chanda said.

"Stay inside," Bornwell said to Alex. "We'll be back soon."

After they left, Mrs. Malaba said, "Explain to me, please, because Bornwell confused me. How did you get lost here?"

"I don't know what happened, really. I was trying to get to the airport, but I got bad directions. And the streets aren't well marked. There are some intersections where there aren't even road signs."

"And your car was stolen. A shame." She shook her head. Despite her plain clothes, she struck Alex as regal, perhaps because of her ramrod-straight posture and her slender wrists and fingers. "I can tell you I almost moved to America this year. But don't say anything to Bornwell. I might still move there!"

"Really, why?"

"I had a man friend, after Bornwell's father was gone, and he moved there two years ago. He wants me to move there; he says he can get me a job and a place to live."

"You should do it!"

"Ah, I will, probably, but not now, not since Bornwell lost his job. But when he gets another one, maybe then." She laughed. "He thinks he's taking care of me, so I let him think it. No harm in it."

"Bornwell will get another job, won't he? He's some kind of genius when it comes to wildlife."

"I know. Strange, with him having grown up here." She gestured out the front window. Several bloated, barefoot children played in the muddy lane, chasing and throwing pebbles at chickens. One of the children had a wire ring fashioned from a coat hanger, and was happily trying to throw it over the heads of his playmates. "That's all the wildlife we see here. Did you see any elephants when you were at Umhlaba?"

"Yeah, I saw a bunch."

She nodded. "I've always wanted to see an elephant."

"You never have?" She shook her head. "You've lived here your whole life and never seen an elephant?"

"No. I've never been to the bush. It's too far, hours and hours, and I've been working, raising Bornwell. Maybe I'll go when I'm an old woman. But I'm already an old woman."

At Kaiser's, Bornwell deposited a small handful of coins into the pay phone and dialed Umhlaba. Franz answered on the first ring.

"Franz, it's Bornwell. I'm sorry to bother you, but there's

a problem with the American guest Alex Stanzis, who was at the lodge last week." Bornwell quickly summarized the situation.

"Ag, man, this is bad," Franz said. "I can't leave right now. There's only me, Tony, and Hennie, and we still haven't finished the burn. But if you can hold out a few days, I'll send someone to pick him up, or just come myself."

"Sir, we need the emergency phone number for his credit card company. It should be on our imprint."

"Give me a minute." Bornwell could hear papers rustling in the background as he looked for the receipt. "Got it."

Bornwell wrote down the number. "Okay sir. Should I call you again?"

"Ya, call me, what's today, Thursday? Call me Sunday."

"Okay."

Franz sensed that Bornwell didn't want to hang up. "I put a call in to Peter van Himst at Sabi Sabi. He sounded very interested in speaking to you about working there."

"Really?"

"Provided you pass your final Parks Board examinations, which of course won't be a problem for you."

"Should I call him?"

"No, let me do it. I'll arrange an interview."

The phone line began to beep. "Sir, I have to go. The phone wants more money. Thank you!"

"Okay son, call me Sunday."

Bornwell returned the handset to its cradle and stared at it for a moment. He walked inside the bar and found Chanda.

"Is the boss going to help?" Chanda said.

"Not right away. He's busy until Sunday. He said to call then."

Chanda frowned. "Shit, you mean we'll have to hide him out until Sunday?"

"Yeah. But the neighbors will see him. They'll talk. Kusasa might hear. But, Chanda — he might get me a job at Sabi Sabi."

"Great, but if Kusasa finds Alex at your house, you'll be Africa's first headless ranger."

"I know. Well, we know this phone works. Let's bring him here and see if he can get a new credit card and passport." Bornwell moved his mouth and the words came out, but his mind was in the bush.

22

Bornwell woke Alex at five a.m. on Friday morning and brought him to the phone. The streets were silent and the air cool and still. Alex reached his credit card company's twenty-four-hour hotline and had his old card cancelled. The woman on the phone told him that it would take two business days for his new card to be mailed to the airport and held by his airline.

"That means it won't get there until Tuesday," he said to Bornwell after he hung up. "So even if Franz can get me on Sunday or Monday, I won't be able to get a hotel or a ticket until Tuesday."

"But at least you'll be away from Kusasa," Bornwell said.

"True. And I could probably get a hotel room without the actual card, just by using the account number. Whatever, first things first: gotta get out of here."

They walked back to Bornwell's house. A few shanties began stirring—lights flickered on, fires were lit—but for the most part, Soweto slept.

"Chanda was telling me something yesterday," Bornwell

said. "He said that in America, the black people are mayors and doctors and lawyers and such."

Alex smiled. "Sure, some of them. They can be whatever they want."

"And the white people don't mind?"

"No, why should they?"

"But we saw on the news a couple of years ago, fighting and rioting between the blacks and whites. What about that?"

"Oh yeah, the Los Angeles riots. That was, uh . . . black people were upset because some white cops beat up a black guy, but when it went to court the jury said they weren't guilty. But the beating was on video, everyone saw it."

"Then why were the cops not guilty?"

"Some legal thing, I don't remember. Self-defense, I think."

Bornwell held up his hand to interrupt Alex, then spoke to an old woman who was setting up a display of home-made pies and pastries in front of her house. He bought two pastries and gave one to Alex.

"Thanks."

"You're welcome. So why did the black people riot, exactly?"

"They were mad. About the decision. They torched their own neighborhood, though, so I don't know what good that did. You'd have to ask them." He took a bite of the pastry. "Holy God, that's good."

Bornwell stopped walking. "What's wrong?" Alex said.

"Shhhhh. Come." He led Alex into a narrow alley and pushed him down behind an overflowing garbage can.

"What is it?" Alex whispered. Bornwell put a finger to his lips. Soon they heard the soft shuffling sounds of footsteps, followed by voices speaking Zulu. The footsteps passed the alley, and the voices quickly faded.

"I can't believe it," Bornwell said. "They were Kusasa, those guys. Can you believe the bad luck, to run into Kusasa at five in the morning?"

"What were they saying?"

"Oh, nothing about you, just talking. Come on."

The men who had walked past had not been Kusasa at all, just a couple of workers on their way to the city. Bornwell merely wanted to scare Alex a little, to make him fully appreciate the danger he was in. He would need Alex's cooperation to keep him concealed, and in order to cooperate, Alex would have to be scared. It was a trick Bornwell learned at the lodge: guests who are a little bit scared tend to follow the rules, whereas the hero types would do stupid things like lag behind their ranger or leave the marked trails, all because they had a false sense of security.

They walked along back streets and alleys as the eastern sky lightened. Alex was visibly shaken now, and didn't say a word. Diesel trucks groaned through their gears in the distance, and shanties began stirring in earnest, people readying themselves for another day of work.

Chanda woke and watched the sun rise over the crumbling shanties as he waited for Bornwell and Alex. He walked down the lane behind his house and stood in line at the water pump as his neighbors filled their buckets. He had nearly reached the front of the line when the rusted handle of the pump snapped off.

"I can fix it," an old man said. "This happens all the time." He bent over and fiddled with the handle, but it kept falling to the ground with a soft clunk. Chanda rolled his eyes and followed the crowd as they walked a half-mile to the next pump.

The elections were only a few weeks away. He and Bornwell never talked about the elections, and he sensed that Bornwell never even thought about them. But he did, and as he watched the sun rise, he thought, maybe after the elections someone will make it so you can get a fucking bucket of water.

23

Alex passed Friday in mind-numbing boredom. He was alone all day. Bornwell's mother left for work at seven, and Bornwell stood all day by the side of a road outside Soweto where white men went to hire black men for daily manual labor and odd jobs. At noon, he helped a man move a new refrigerator into his house in Bryanston for ten rand, but that was the only work he got. In the evening, Bornwell and Alex played cards for three hours. Bornwell noticed the American was more talkative than usual, and reluctant to let the game end.

Bornwell woke in the middle of the night. He sat up in bed. Alex slept soundly on a cot next to him. Bornwell walked to the window and peered out. A few streetlights burned in the distance, casting orange cones of light into the street. He looked into the sky — no stars. Already it was a distant memory, but he remembered when he would awaken late at night at Umhlaba, often to the sound of an animal moving through the bush near his hut. Once, he woke and looked out of his window directly into the face of an enormous kudu. Now his view was cones of buzzing light splashing into broken roads.

Chanda came over early on Saturday morning. "Stay out of sight," Bornwell said to Alex. "Chanda and I have to go out."

"Where are you guys going?"

"We're going to a football match. Pirates against Kaiser Chiefs. It's the biggest game of the year."

Alex sagged. "So I have to sit around here all day again?"

"There's nothing else we can do. Kusasa will be all over the place because of the match."

Chanda pulled Bornwell aside. "I was thinking of something on the way over here," he said. "What if Ekeke could get him onto the team bus after the game? They're going back to a hotel in Joburg right after the game, because they have to play Cape Town Spurs on Tuesday."

Bornwell shook his head. "Come on. Even if Ekeke went along with it, the bosses never would. Sneak a man onto the bus of Orlando Pirates?"

"Ekeke would do it. And the manager wouldn't care. Ekeke could tell him Alex is a sportswriter or something."

Bornwell looked over at Alex. He whispered to Chanda in Zulu. "A sportswriter, sure. Covered with mud!"

Chanda scratched his head. "Ah, we'll give him one of my shirts." Bornwell looked doubtful. "Hey man, it's worth a try. You want him sitting around here forever? What if your boss can't come? David's gonna find him here sooner or later. At least this way we're doing something about it. And I'll tell you one thing: it will work or it won't, but either way we won't have this problem much longer." They looked at Alex. "For better or worse."

Bornwell smiled grimly. "Ah, shit. I guess it's worth a try." In English, he said to Alex, "You're coming to the game with us. We might be able to get you on a bus to Johannesburg."

Alex leapt to his feet. "Hell yeah, let's go!"

The road to the stadium winds past deserted lots where, on match days, children and teenagers play soccer amid great clouds of orange dust. It's not a pretty neighborhood, but the reality of the townships—the broken glass and garbage, the old tires, the overgrown weeds and boarded windows—can be ignored, temporarily at least, in favor of a simple game of soccer.

Two hours before the game, the road began filling up with men and boys who moved slowly, shoulder to shoulder, along the wide, dusty lane. The games in the lots continued in earnest, the boys shouting aloud as they gained possession of the ball: "I'm Marks Maponyane!" "I'm Doctor Khumalo!" They called the names of their heroes, the men who even now were preparing nervously in the dressing rooms beneath the unsteady bulk of the old wooden stadium.

Chanda, Bornwell, and Alex walked quickly down the road. "How are they not going to see me? I'm the only white guy here!" Alex said.

"Don't worry," said Bornwell, who was very worried indeed. "Just keep low. I don't see them anywhere."

"Anyway, look at you," Chanda said. Alex's expensive clothes had not been made to withstand the battering they had taken, and they'd begun to unravel. "You're starting to fit in nicely."

"Maybe they'll skip this match?" Bornwell said.

"Oh come on, Pirates versus Chiefs? They'll be here," Chanda said. "But they all sit behind the east goal. We'll just stay at the other end."

"Sounds easy enough," said Alex.

"I just hope Ekeke can help us," Chanda said.

Bornwell put a hand on Chanda's shoulder and stopped him. "What do you mean, you hope? Earlier you said he'd be happy to help!"

"Yes, well, but I forgot that he's bound to be nervous before such a big match."

"Then why don't you just wait until after the match to ask him?"

Chanda waved suddenly to a young boy who called his name, then ran through the crowd of men. "Yeah, that's what I'll do. After the game."

The stadium was in sight. Chanda whispered in Zulu to Bornwell. "Do you think he remembers he said he was going to reward us for our help?"

"Yes, I'm sure he does."

Chanda snorted.

They neared the entrance gate. Bornwell told Alex to walk close behind them and to keep his head down. Soon the crowd was tight against them, pushing forward and rocking from side to side. A small group in front of them broke into song, a rhythmic chant that swept back through the crowd and reverberated across the street. The noise around Alex was deafening as everyone, now even Bornwell and Chanda, sang together as one voice. Firecrackers popped and air horns cried out intermittently. Men waved giant white flags adorned with the black skull-and-crossbones emblem of the Pirates. Small boys somehow found gaps in the massed bodies and streaked through the crowd, laughing and flashing toothy smiles at the older men who grumbled at them.

At the gate Chanda produced the three tickets. Inside the stadium they wedged their way into the crowd behind the west goal, where the fans competed for a tiny piece of splintered bleacher. Bornwell and Chanda protectively flanked Alex. Chanda pointed across the stadium: Kusasa had arrived, claiming their usual territory behind the east goal. They waved flags and sang in a voice that carried to the children still playing in the vacant lots, the children who would soon abandon their games and crawl through the holes they always found in the stadium's fence.

"There's so many," Bornwell said.

"There's a lot, but most of them just like to sing the Kusasa songs and wear the colors. Most of them wouldn't hurt a rat."

"How do you tell the ones who would from the ones who wouldn't?" Alex said.

Chanda laughed. "That's the hard part."

They gave up hope of passing Alex off as a reporter when they saw the media ensconced in a box atop the east end of the stadium, directly above and behind Kusasa. Anyway, most of the fans near them ignored Alex. "If anybody asks who you are," Chanda said to him, "just tell them you're Gavin Lane's brother."

"Who's Gavin Lane?"

"He's the only white man that plays for Pirates."

The vast crowd suddenly burst into shrieking whistles of scorn as the orange-clad Kaiser Chiefs entered the field in a solemn single file. The players broke off and began warming up at the far end of the field, where the Kusasa masses showered them with abuse.

"They don't like those guys, do they?" Alex said.

"Everybody around here hates the Chiefs," Chanda said.

Then the noise of the crowd changed, swelled, grew deeper, and the old men in felt hats and the boys in torn shirts erupted into ardent cheers as Pirates appeared on the field, dazzling in their white shirts under the African sun. Bornwell and Chanda forgot for a moment the burden sitting between them, and leapt up and down and shouted along with forty thousand Pirates fans all around the stadium. Alex laughed. He'd never seen serious, reserved Bornwell display so much excitement.

"It's been three years since I've been to a Pirates match!" Bornwell said by way of explanation, when he noticed Alex's amusement.

The game began, and the noise of the crowd rose and fell with every pass, tackle, and shot. Despite the support of their huge crowd, Pirates began the match poorly. They scrambled frantically about the pitch, trying to win possession of the ball as Chiefs calmly stroked it from teammate to teammate. They were dangerous on the attack, dribbling and passing through the static Pirates' defense time and again, launching threatening shots at the Pirates' goal. Only the inspired athletics of the Orlando goalkeeper kept the match scoreless.

"Looks bad, looks bad," said an older man in front of Bornwell.

"It's okay, Pops; they always start slowly," Chanda said.

But a moment later, Chiefs' star Doctor Khumalo sliced between two defenders and lashed a rising twenty-yard shot into the roof of the Pirates' net. The huge crowd groaned and then fell silent, except for a small group of Chiefs' fans in a corner of the stadium. They stood and cheered somewhat reservedly, mindful of their surroundings.

Alex grew bored. He kept an eye on Kusasa, but they were too far away to be a threat. "How long until halftime?" he said.

"Not long," Chanda said tersely. He and Bornwell had grown quiet since the goal.

Late in the first half, just when the grumbles of the Pirates fans had reached an apex, the home team forced a terrific scramble right in front of the Chiefs' goal. When a Pirates player finally prodded the ball into the net, the once-dormant crowd exploded into extravagant celebration, and songs echoed around the stadium again. Even Alex was impressed by this spectacle, which lasted until the referee blew his whistle for halftime.

During the intermission, Bornwell and Chanda talked about how to approach Ekeke after the match, while Alex distractedly watched men in the crowd urinating off the top row of the stands. He glanced across the field at the Kusasa crowd.

"Hey, are those Kusasa guys coming this way?"

"No, don't worry," Bornwell said without looking.

"Goddamit, they are! Look!"

Chanda slapped Bornwell on the arm. "How could I forget? They always move at halftime to the goal Pirates are attacking!"

The white-shirted Kusasa moved slowly in a long line along the fence that surrounded the playing field. The first of them were still seventy yards away, but they pushed forward steadily.

"We have to go right now," Bornwell said. He prodded Alex, and they started down the bleachers. But Chanda thought they might meet Kusasa head-on that way. They turned around and climbed to the top of the stadium, then clambered down a rickety flight of stairs to the ground. They walked with measured strides, trying to look unhurried, when in fact they could barely restrain themselves from sprinting. At the exit gate, Chanda caught the eye of a young man smoking a cigarette next to the gate. He had a scruffy beard with three or four dreadlocks twisted into it. He looked at Alex and then back at Chanda, puzzled. Then an expression of recognition passed across his pockmarked face, and he threw his cigarette to the ground and walked back into the stadium.

"That guy at the gate was Kusasa," Chanda said once they were outside.

"He didn't have the shirt," Bornwell said.

"I know, but I remember him from the other day, when David gave me the tickets. I remember his beard. He's probably running to get others."

"Shit!" He turned to Alex. "Can you run?"

"Yeah, man. I run every day at home. But these shoes —"

"Forget the shoes, let's get moving, seriously," Chanda said.

The three of them ran back past the vacant lots and makeshift soccer fields, empty now, and through the shanties surrounding Orlando. The hum of the crowd faded as they jogged through the dusty streets. Chanda looked over his shoulder and saw several white-shirted men tearing out of the stadium gate at a full sprint. "They're coming!" he screamed. They ran down the main street, past alleys, stores, and shacks. "Let's hide and let them run past!" Chanda said.

"Not yet!" Bornwell said.

Chanda dropped two, then four, then six paces behind Alex and Bornwell. "Let's hide! I can't go much farther!" Chanda panted. Alex was a frequent jogger, and Bornwell had the requisite fitness of a ranger, but Chanda never exercised and was about thirty pounds overweight.

"Now, let's hide now!" Chanda moaned.

Bornwell looked over his shoulder. He couldn't see the men because he was leading them through a grid of shanties, turning randomly. The men were close, but they weren't always in sight. He waited until they turned a sharp corner. "Okay!" Bornwell shouted. "Here!" They rumbled past a startled old man standing in the street with a rake in his hands, and dived into a small shanty.

They sat without speaking, gasping great hot breaths and wiping the sweat off their faces, peering out at the street through gaps in the tin panels. Bornwell heard a noise behind them and turned. An old woman knelt close to them and beckoned with one finger. They followed her to the back of the shanty, where she had a large kitchen table. She lifted the tablecloth that hung to the floor, and they crawled under it. She dropped the cloth and whispered, "Don't move."

Chanda parted the cloth just enough to see into the street. He saw the Kusasa men run past without slowing down, but moments later they all heard shouting.

A loud voice, speaking Zulu, rang out. "You must have seen them, old man. Where'd they go?" Chanda leaned out to see the speaker. He was a heavily muscled man with a red sash tied around his python-like biceps.

"Yeah man, I saw them," the old man said. "They ran right on by me. That way." He pointed down the long, empty street.

"Nah, they must have hid," said the Kusasa man with the dreads in his beard.

"Don't lie to me," the big Kusasa man said.

"I'm not," the old man said simply. He inadvertently glanced at them and met Chanda's eye, then continued raking.

"Oh Christ, he's going to give us away," Alex whispered.

"Shut up, shut up," Bornwell hissed.

The Kusasa men—eight in all—crowded around the old man. One of them, a wiry boy no more than sixteen, knocked the rake from his hands.

"Last chance," the big man said. "Where are they?"

Bornwell tensed. "Get ready," he whispered. "There's a back door."

The old woman who hid them walked into the street. "What's this? What's this?" she wailed. "You leave him alone!"

Some of the Kusasa were startled and stepped back from the old man. A few nodded to her politely. She screamed at the big man, who smiled patiently at her. Then he gathered the old man by the front of his shirt and smacked him across the face with the back of his hand—not violently, but hard enough to send his crooked glasses flying into the street.

"Ah fuck," Bornwell moaned.

"They're gonna rat us out now," Alex said.

Bornwell whirled on Alex. "That old man is getting beaten because of you!"

"Hey, it wasn't my idea to go to a fucking soccer game!"

"Shh!" Chanda hissed. He was still out of breath from the run, and he gasped as he whispered. "Shut up you idiots! Shut up you stupid American asshole!"

In the street, the old man seemed strangely disaffected. He retrieved his glasses and his rake, and even resumed scratching at the pebbly ground. The old woman continued to rail at the Kusasa men.

"Okay, yes, okay," the big man said to the woman. He spoke to the other men, and they began walking back to the stadium. The old man smiled at his wife and continued his raking. Just then the lanky youth who'd knocked the man's rake out of his hands ran back and pushed him to the ground, then delivered a wild kick to his stomach. The woman wailed, ran to her husband, and screamed after the kid, who ran laughing back to his companions.

Bornwell waited until the Kusasa were gone, then ran to the man in the street. "Are you all right? Sir?" He and the woman helped the man to his feet. A trickle of blood dropped from a scrape on his forehead. The woman dabbed at it with her hand. The man laughed with his mouth wide open, displaying no more than five teeth jutting starkly from his gums. "Eh, the hell with them boys!"

"Sir, thank you! We're sorry this happened," Chanda said, joining them in the street.

"Eh, it's okay. I don't like those boys. Always they're coming here and fighting, scaring the old people, going after the boys to make join. The hell with them."

"Well, thanks again, sir. Go well," Bornwell said.

"Stay well. You better get that white man out of here."

"We're trying, sir."

25

"It would have worked," Chanda lamented as they walked along back streets to Bornwell's house. "Ekeke would have come through for us."

"Even so, we'll want to go to the airport with him, if we want to get any money out of it," Bornwell said in Zulu.

Chanda answered him in that language. "You don't trust him? You don't think he'll come through with the money?"

Bornwell shrugged. "I don't know. He's desperate. I think he might just forget."

"Come on you guys, speak English," Alex whined.

"We were just talking about the game," Bornwell said.

They crouched and hid a few times when they saw groups of men in the streets, but the Kusasa were all still at the game. They reached Bornwell's house and sat in the backyard. Alex was wracked by a brief bout of chills. "Wow," he said. "God. This is the first time I've been able to take a deep breath all day."

Chanda glared at him and shook his head, but the American didn't notice.

"So what did I tell you about Chiefs' offside trap?" he said to Bornwell. "Almost impossible to break down, isn't it?"

"Yeah, but when you do break it down, you've got them at your mercy."

"Too bad the linesman kept calling us offside, though."

Alex stood and stretched his arms above his head. He walked the perimeter of the small yard while Chanda and Bornwell talked about the game, and sat back down. He waited for a lull in their conversation, then said, "Are you guys going to go to Kaiser's tonight?"

Chanda said, "Maybe, why?"

"I could really use a beer. Maybe you could bring back a couple for me."

Chanda looked at Alex in astonishment, then pointed at him and in Zulu said to Bornwell, "You know, we really are fucked now. We can't go to Kaiser's tonight, or ever again! This fucker has ruined it for us! Once those toadies tell David that you and me were with him, we're history."

Bornwell nodded. He crossed his legs and rested his chin in his hands. "I better call Franz again and tell him it's gotten worse. I'll go tonight."

"I better get home," Chanda said. "I haven't seen Mother in days, it seems." He stood to leave.

Alex stood with him. "I've been meaning to ask: does 'Kusasa' mean anything in English?"

"It means 'tomorrow,'" Chanda said.

"Tomorrow. I guess it's supposed to be visionary," Alex said.

Bornwell smiled. "Supposed to be."

"Shit, guys, I'm sorry I got you all involved in this," Alex said. "I know you'd rather be out chasing girls." He playfully poked Chanda in the stomach. "Whoa, man. Better do some more sit-ups."

"What?" Chanda said.

"Did you hear him huffing and puffing when we were running?" Alex said to Bornwell. "I thought he was gonna fucking die on us!"

Chanda laughed and patted his stomach. "Don't worry about me. This is a beautiful body right here."

"So where are the girls? You guys getting any action?" Alex asked.

"I had a girl for a while, but . . ." Chanda held up his hands and smiled.

"But now you've got Bornwell? Damn, man, that's a downgrade."

Chanda's smile vanished. "What do you mean?"

"Well, dude! You guys engaged, or what? You haven't been apart since—"

Chanda grabbed Alex at the shoulder. "You think that's *funny?*"

"He didn't mean anything, Chanda," Bornwell said, quickly stepping in front of his cousin and pulling his hand away from Alex.

"Yeah man, relax. I'm just kidding with you," Alex said. "No offense."

"It's not the kind of thing we make jokes about," Bornwell explained.

"Okay. My fault." He held out his hand. Chanda ignored it for a moment, but then exchanged a quick slap with Alex. "Okay. Cool."

"Yeah," Chanda muttered.

Chanda stayed at home the rest of the day, and all day Sunday. To pacify his mother, he did all of his brothers' and sisters' chores for them, then helped her with the wash. Bornwell came over on Sunday, but Chanda didn't want to see or hear about Alex, and he told his mother to tell Bornwell he was too busy with chores to see him.

Chanda's father worked for months at a time in the mines outside the city. Chanda wasn't sure when he would be coming home again. He'd received a letter from him a week ago, and, sitting cross-legged in the middle of the kitchen area, he reread it for the hundredth time:

Chanda,

Hello son! I hope you are well and looking after mother. The work has not been so hard these days and I'll try to come home soon I think. My contract ends at the end of the month but it might be extended for a longer. If you have heard about the trouble here, it's not so bad really. The white soldiers are here all day when we are down the mines, but when we come home at night they leave and there is nobody there for us when Inkatha come. But so far they haven't caused problems here, just handed out papers. Maybe because so many of the men in the dorm are already with Inkatha. As for me I just want hot water in the shower at night! It is so usually cold. I cant believe Pirates lost to Cape Town Spurs last week! At home! Did you see the game? I cant remember such a so bad season in so long. Well I have to go post this now. Stay well and I will see you soon.

With love,
Father

Chanda thought about the life his father was leading, working ten to twelve hours a day in the mines, sending home almost all of the money he made to support a family he almost never saw. He wondered if his father ever wanted to go out for a beer or see a movie or a soccer game. He guessed his father probably didn't allow himself to think of such things. His father was a hard worker.

Chanda was not. He knew it, yet didn't feel guilty about it. Hard work didn't pay off, not in Soweto. His father had worked hard all his life, and all it had gotten him was month after month in a filthy cold-water hostel with a hundred other men.

There was a lot of talk in Soweto about how things would be in the "new" South Africa: that is, after the elections. Many people weren't convinced that life would change much, but most felt that, if nothing else, the whites would be forced to pay better wages to black people who worked for them. That meant his parents, and Bornwell's mother, would be a little better off.

How it would affect him, he was less sure. He didn't have a job at the moment. He was tired of chasing after people, both black and white, and asking for a job. It was demeaning. He wanted to be the one people came to. He wanted people to ask him for jobs. But how that could happen he couldn't imagine. He thought of Alex Stanzis, how he had everything in the world and just needed to get out of Soweto to get back to it, and he thought of how hard he and Bornwell were trying to help him, even though they had nowhere else to go.

For the first time in his young life, the hopelessness that gripped the regulars he drank with at Kaiser's, men twice his age, began to resonate within him. Sunday evening he went to see David Themba.

26

He found them gathered near the secondary school in West Orlando. They stood across the street from a group of policemen. He approached them nervously. He didn't see David. They ignored him at first, thinking he would walk past, but when he didn't, someone said, "What do you want?"

"I'm looking for David."

"Why?"

"He gave me tickets to the Pirates-Chiefs match. I wanted to thank him."

"He's not here."

"Okay. I'll come back later."

He started to walk away. Someone said, "Hey man." Chanda turned around. It was the big goon with the red sash around his upper arm. "You're the one who's supposed to be looking for the white man."

Chanda nodded. He saw the others now look at him with interest. He stepped back involuntarily. "I haven't seen him," he said.

"But you went to the match yesterday. Instead of looking for him."

"David told me to go. He gave me the tickets. I didn't want to insult him by not going."

"Eh-heh. What's your name?"

"Chanda."

The big man stepped back and took off his sunglasses. He wiped them with the front of his shirt and put them back on, even though it was almost dark. His arm muscles rippled like coiled vipers. "I'm Steve Lekoelea. I'm gonna tell David you're still looking for the white man, okay?"

"Uh, no, don't tell him that."

"Why not?"

The others edged closer to Chanda, but not in a threatening way. They just wanted to hear what he had to say. Chanda scanned Steve's face.

"Let me talk to David," he said.

27

Bornwell woke suddenly. He looked out his window. Chanda stood there tapping at the glass. Bornwell lifted the window.

"Man, where've you been? I looked for you today," Bornwell said.

"Great news! Get Alex. Wake him up. I found a guy with a car who'll take him to the airport right now, for just fifty rand, and he'll even let us pay him later, when we get the money."

"You found a guy? Who?"

"Him." Chanda pointed behind him at a skinny man leaning against a blue Honda.

"Who is he?" Bornwell asked.

"What's it matter? Come on man, get Alex."

Bornwell withdrew from the window, but then returned. "It matters. If something happens to Alex, Franz might get in trouble for it."

Chanda groaned. "We can trust this guy, okay? He

knows he doesn't get his fifty rand unless he gets Alex to the airport."

"Let me talk to him," Bornwell said.

"Man, I told—"

"I talk to him, or Alex doesn't get in that car."

"Okay, okay, just don't scare him off," Chanda said. He turned to the man. "Come here, Andele."

As soon as the man joined Chanda, Bornwell saw that he was drunk. "Bornwell, this is Andele. What's your last name, brother?"

"Celi. Andele Celi," the man said. Bornwell didn't say anything. Andele filled the silence by laughing nervously.

"No way," Bornwell said.

"What! He—"

"He's drunk. No disrespect to you, sir," Bornwell said. "But I can't put my friend in your car if you're drunk."

"I'll take him in the morning, then, sir," Andele said, bowing politely. "I'll sleep, and then come for him in the morning?"

Andele and Chanda both looked hopefully up at Bornwell. He nodded.

"Good, good, man. Okay. We'll see you in the morning," Chanda said. They started to walk to Andele's car. Bornwell reached from the window and grabbed Chanda's shoulder.

"Hey man. Good job, so long as this guy works out."

"Sure, cousin. You knew I'd take care of it."

28

"**A**ll I want to know," David said, "is what you thought of the soccer game."

Alex shook his head and laughed. "That's it?" He looked around him. David sat next to him on a hard wooden bench in the middle of a dark room. Steve Lekoelea stood right behind David. A dozen other Kusasa sat in front of the bench. Alex saw guns—Steve had one, David had one, a kid who looked no more than thirteen was positively bristling with them. Nobody had touched him, or threatened him, but he knew he wasn't free to get up and walk out, either.

"That's it. What did you think?"

"Well . . ." he raised his palms and shrugged. "I didn't get to see the whole game."

"You missed a good one," David said. "Complete domination by Pirates in the second half, after the bad start that you saw."

"Glad to hear it," Alex said politely. "I understand the Pirates are the local favorites?"

"They're all most people here have. We've followed—"

"Are you kidnapping me?" Alex said. "Is that the deal here? Because you are making one hell of a fucking mistake. I'm an American citizen. Do you know what that means? It means — "

"Yes, I do know what that means. That's what I want to talk to you about. That's why you're here. This isn't a kidnapping. You can go, if you want."

"Fine." Alex stood up. "I'm going."

"Be my guest. But didn't Chanda tell you I wasn't the only one looking for you? You go out there, there's a happy little group called APF — Azanian People's Front. They will kill you, man. They don't want your money. They'll just kill you for the attention it will bring them."

"So what? I don't have any money. Not a dime. Anyway, are my chances any better here?" Alex said.

"Nobody's going to touch you here. Nobody besides me is even going to talk to you. If you help me out with what I want, I'll get you wherever you need to go."

"What do you want?"

David stood. He motioned for Steve and the others to back away, then paced in front of Alex. "Can I tell you one thing at a time? If I hit you with it all at once, you won't understand, or it won't make sense." He gestured to Steve, who handed him a joint. David lit it and offered it to Alex, who shook his head.

"Look, man. This country is going through changes. Maybe you heard?" Alex offered no reply. "Maybe you don't care. But people here, these guys — " he spread his arms " — we got nothing. But we're doing something about it. It isn't about violence, and being a gang. I'm trying to build something that — "

"Can you skip the politics, dude? I don't give a shit about sociology. What do you want from me?"

David nodded. "Chanda told me you were like that. If I was worried about what these guys thought of me, I might not let you get away with it."

Alex remembered the guns. "Sorry. I'm just nervous. It would help if I knew — "

"We've got to get you a decent suit," David said.

29

"It's been two days," Bornwell said. "We should have heard from Alex by now."

"Yeah, I've gotta tell you something about that," Chanda said. He glanced at Bornwell, then quickly looked away. "I should have told you already. I'm sorry, man. Before I say anything, Alex is gonna be fine. David isn't going to hurt him."

"What the fuck are you . . ." Bornwell rose from his chair, then slumped back into it. "You sent Alex to David. That driver—"

"Andele. Yeah, he's one of David's guys."

Bornwell sighed. "Alex never did anything to you, and you fucked him over. Me, too. Maybe even Franz, if this gets out."

"No, man. I talked to David. I swear—he just wants to use Alex at some rally. He's going to have Alex pretend to be a supporter from an American political group."

"What the hell for? That's the stupidest—"

"And then he's going to take Alex to the airport himself. And since we helped him, David's going to take care of both of us."

Bornwell put his hands over his face. "Jesus, Chanda. You sent him right to David. You know he's not going to agree to any of this. What's David going to do then?"

"No, man, really. David has it all worked out."

"Are you working for David now? Is that it? Joining the Revolution? Shit." Bornwell sighed and stood. "Okay, where are they?"

"How should I know? Nobody ever knows where David is."

"I want to know. I'm going to go see him and make sure Alex is okay. If he isn't, I'm getting the police."

Chanda laughed. "You send the police to David, and he'll never forget it! Man, you'll be dead!"

"What fucking choice do I have? Just tell me where he is."

"Okay, fine. I'll take you there myself. But no police, man. Swear it."

"Alright, no police. Unless he's hurt Alex."

30

David and Alex sat alone behind the small house. Inside, Steve and the others waited, listening to Radio Soweto and smoking.

"It's called the Soweto Freedom Summit," David said. "It's a sort of political fair. There's going to be speeches from ANC and Inkatha representatives, plus a few other, smaller organizations. I'm speaking there. Just a ten-minute speech, an introduction. What I want is for you to speak, too."

"What the hell do I know about it?"

"I'll tell you what to say. Just a few words. You're going to be like this guy." He handed Alex a newspaper and pointed at a small headline: AMERICAN EDUCATOR TO SPEAK AT SOWETO FREEDOM SUMMIT. "He's going to talk about the university's role in political movements. You'll talk about something a lot more generic. I'll write it up — it'll be easy to remember," he said, cutting off Alex's protest. "You can use notes. I'll say my piece, you'll give me your support — that's it."

Alex smiled. "You have no idea how much I'm the wrong guy for this. I don't know anything about your causes or issues. I don't even know anything about your country. What if people start asking me questions?"

"If you read what I write, people are going to stand up and cheer for you. Has that ever happened to you before?"

"Not since breakfast," Alex said.

David stood. "I don't get your jokes," he said.

"I'm just trying to — stay calm, I guess."

"Look around you, man," David said. He pointed at a silty ditch full of garbage and mud. "That's sewage. Look at that house." He pointed at a shanty made from a patchwork of irregular shapes of plywood and tin. "Nine people live there. Seven of them kids, under ten years old. All of them sick almost all the time. No heat in winter, the rain comes in. So stay calm, yes. But this isn't the place for jokes."

31

"Thank you very much," Alex said. The crowd stopped clapping. He looked out at the faces — more than he expected — and coughed nervously. The crowd filled the grass field in front of the Mzimhilope Hostel. Teenagers and young men crowded the area in front of the speaker's platform. Alex made eye contact with a young man sitting just below his feet. He smiled and nodded at him, but the young man didn't return the greeting.

"Thank you," Alex said again. He shuffled his note cards and looked over at David. David nodded at him.

"America is a rich and powerful country," he began. "But I am here today because I want to be part of your strength — the strength of passion. The strength of commitment. The strength of people who are ready to embrace change!"

Some in the crowd clapped. "Thank you. I'm also here because I want to give my official support to David Themba and Kusasa. All of us in the American Freedom Foundation are excited about his vision for Sowetans. Remember to pick up a leaflet before you leave." He held up a lemon-yellow flyer. "It's got all the information you need."

People in the crowd fanned themselves. Alex looked over at David again. David was inspecting his fingernails.

"Some of you think you're doing enough just by being here today. It's a start, but it's not enough. Which of these groups, which of these political parties, are inviting you to join them right here, today, and start working for change?" Alex said, his voice swelling with confidence. "The big parties just want your vote. David wants your vote!"

David stiffened in his chair. He glared at Alex. A few muffled laughs came from the audience.

"I mean, your sweat! David wants your sweat next to his. Sweat together in the streets of Soweto for clean water, for a ban on unauthorized police searches, for . . ." Alex fumbled with his notes. "Township representation in the new government. And, uh, a brighter future for us all. Thank you."

The audience clapped politely.

32

"'A brighter future for us all'? Where did that come from?" David said.

"I don't know. I panicked a little. I couldn't find the last page of my notes. I told you I was going to be nervous! But how about the rest of it? How was I?"

"Yeah, it was okay. You did fine, yeah. Alright. So we've got to take you to the airport now, right? You can keep the suit."

"What have you got next?" Alex said.

"What do you mean?"

"I mean, what's next? Are there going to be more rallies?"

David shook his head. "You really want to know?"

"Yeah, I mean . . ." Alex shrugged. "I'm just curious."

David nodded. "No more rallies, at least for now. They're good for the ego, but they don't really accomplish much. We're going to start publishing a newsletter, just a two-page thing, and we'll give it away free."

"That's a great idea! When I was in college, me and a couple of guys put out a little newsletter every month. It was a parody of the official student newspaper, which really sucked. We had, like, a fake top ten songs list that, you know, sort of mocked all the songs that were popular then. Like, we had 'Sez You, Sez Yo Mama,' instead of 'Say You, Say Me,' by Lionel Richie, you know?"

David stared at Alex for a few seconds before speaking. "I really have no idea what you're talking about, man," he said.

33

C handa paused in front of the door. He raised a fist, looked at Bornwell for support, then rapped on the door three times. "This is crazy," Chanda muttered.

"Don't worry," Bornwell whispered. "Just remember to —"

Steve Lekoelea answered the door and scowled fiercely. "Who the fuck are you?" he demanded. "Oh, yeah . . . Chanda." Steve stood a head taller than Chanda. He pointed over him at Bornwell. "Who is this? What are you doing bringing a stranger here?"

"It's okay," Chanda said. "David knows him. This is Bornwell. He's my cousin."

"Hello," Bornwell said weakly. Steve didn't look at him. "What do you want?"

"David," Chanda said. "Can we see him?"

"Not here."

"Oh. Alright."

Steve relaxed his glare just a little. "He's gone to see his brother."

"Oh, good. Stephen, right? Good," Chanda said.

"Yeah," Steve said. "It does him good, talking to Stephen. It takes his mind off being sick."

"So okay, we'll come back—"

"Where's the American?" Bornwell asked.

Steve hardened again. "What American?"

"Alex Stanzis. The white man Chanda brought to you last week."

Steve stepped out of the door, pushed past Chanda, and loomed over Bornwell. "Chanda," he said evenly, staring down at Bornwell, "I don't know who this shrimp is, but I'm not happy he's here, and I don't like him asking questions of me."

"I'm sorry, Steve, but it's okay, really. See, we just want to make sure the American did his job for David. I feel responsible. I want to make sure David is happy."

"David is not happy," Steve said. "The American fucked up. You two fucked up."

Chanda and Bornwell involuntarily backed up a step. Steve noticed. He stepped forward and swelled his chest. "David's going to want to talk to you about this," he growled.

"But where is the American?" Bornwell said. "I'm sorry, but I have to know if he is okay. Otherwise I'll have to . . ." Chanda turned and looked at Bornwell, his eyes wide. He shook his head no, but Bornwell ignored him. "To call the police."

A heavy silence hung over the three of them. Steve smiled. Chanda didn't like the look of it. He smiled back at Steve. "No, don't worry, nobody's calling the police. He just—"

Steve suddenly pushed Chanda to one side and lunged for Bornwell with his right arm. Bornwell jumped back, out of his reach. Steve took one step, paused, and then ran at Bornwell, who nimbly turned and ran. Chanda followed, and ran right into Steve's back when the big man decided not to chase Bornwell. Chanda rolled to his feet and ducked just in time to evade Steve's right fist. He ran in the direction opposite to where Bornwell had gone. Steve stood between the two of them, Chanda twenty yards to his right, Bornwell twenty to his left.

"David is going to be angry about this," Chanda said, his voice betraying his optimism. "I've helped him, and you're attacking me?!?"

"David is angry, but not at me," Steve said. He shifted his eyes from one to the other. "He told me to take care of you when he left. If I don't get you today, I'll get you tomorrow. Or the day after."

Chanda and Bornwell kept backing away slowly. Steve made a final dash at Bornwell, but his bulk slowed him, and Bornwell easily outran him.

"I'll fucking take care of both of you soon enough!" Steve yelled after them. "I won't forget this!"

"I've got a stepbrother in Cape Town," Chanda said. "He's got his own house. Maybe we could stay with him for a while."

Bornwell thought for a moment. "Of all your ideas, Chanda, that one is, by far . . ."

"Yeah?"

"The most recent."

"Very funny. You have a better idea?"

Bornwell said, "Wait a sec, I'll be right back." He went back in his house and emerged a minute later with a scrap of paper. "I could call Sara. Maybe we could go stay with her for a while. You try to make peace with David, and if he doesn't take it well, we'll just get out of town."

"Who's Sara?"

"Sara, come on, I've told you about her. The girl I worked with, the smart one."

"Oh, the ranger's daughter?"

"Yeah. She gave me her number when I left. She said I

could stay at her place in Bosbokrand if I had interviews with other lodges."

"We could go there, I guess. But let's go to Cape Town first. I've never been there."

"I've been saying all this time you need to see more of the country anyway. Fat city boy."

"Fat for now, until Steve carves off a piece of me. I guess I'll go try to see David in a few days." Chanda sighed. "If I could just find a way around that goon Steve."

"Want me to go with you?"

"Nah. He doesn't really know you. It's better if you keep away from him. Man, I just knew that American was going to be trouble."

"Did I not tell you the guy was an idiot?"

"No lectures, professor," Chanda said. He slapped Bornwell on the arm. "Now, what are we supposed to do about money?" he said.

"I have some. They gave me some when they fired me from the lodge. I was hoping to save it until I got another job, but it'll do me more good this way. We'll have to be really careful with it though. We'll have to watch every rand."

Shouting came from the lane behind Bornwell's house. They turned and saw two young boys fighting. The boys were small and skinny but fought with frightening intensity, throwing wild punches and wailing in anger and terror. Bornwell rolled his eyes and said, "Heavyweight title fight!"

"Settle down!" Chanda shouted at the boys, but they ignored him.

"It's okay, those two are always fighting."

But Chanda shook his head and ran to the boys. He pushed them apart, slapped each on the side of the head, and sent them away, where they soon resumed playing peacefully.

35

From the bus's high vantage point, Chanda could see over the fences and into the fields, some tended but most vacant, vast acres of waving grass extending to the lumpy horizon, broken in only a few places by trees. He leaned back in his seat and watched the landscape roll by.

"So David wouldn't even talk to you?" Bornwell asked.

Chanda groaned.

"I know, you don't want to talk about it. But I'd like to know—"

"He blew me off, okay? I went to see him, and they said he didn't want to see anyone. Said he was sick." He shrugged. "Maybe he really was. Still, you'd think he'd talk to me. I sent him Alex."

"Maybe he's really mad, like Steve said?"

"Why would he be? I think it's just Steve. He hated me the first time I met him."

"Well, that guy's a psycho anyway," Bornwell said.

The trip took two days. Chanda slept most of the time,

while Bornwell fidgeted and tried to read a field guide to Southern African reptiles. In Cape Town, they found lodging in a hostel not far from the Victoria & Albert Waterfront, a collection of pricey shops and restaurants surrounding an attractive marina. They spent most of their first few days there, looking halfheartedly for the stepbrother, smiling at the girls, and ignoring the glares of security guards.

"So many rich people," Chanda said as they walked through the crowds. "Smooth roads for the cars, and sidewalks to walk on. It's another world."

"It's not so different from Joburg," Bornwell said.

Chanda shrugged. "Maybe, but you look around Joburg and it's just tall buildings. Look here—flowerbeds, parks. Mountains on one side, the entire ocean on the other."

"It's beautiful."

"But I doubt it's any better than home," Chanda said as an afterthought. "Pretty scenes are good for the soul, but they don't do shit for your wallet."

"We could get jobs here, if you want to stay," Bornwell said.

"You think? Doing what?"

"We could find something. Every restaurant needs dishwashers. Every store needs someone to sweep the floor."

"All my wildest dreams come true."

"Only for a short time."

"No thanks. But I did hear about something—I saw an advert—a supervisor training program, in Kimberley. It didn't sound bad."

"I thought you hated everything about the mines?"

"I know. David says they're a death sentence. But my father doesn't seem to mind so much. Maybe if you're a supervisor, it isn't so bad."

"Maybe not. Anyway, I'll be getting on with another lodge soon, and by then it'll be safe for you to go home."

Chanda laughed. "It'll never be safe, not as long as David has Steve around. This isn't a solution, it's just stalling. But that's okay." He pointed across the street, at the girls shopping in the stores. "They'll have to kill me to stop me from living."

"That's so corny."

They learned Cape Town's bus routes and started spending their days at the beaches at the foot of rocky hills. The girls often went topless at Clifton Beach, but Llandudno was their favorite—more remote, less crowded. They stretched out across great rounded boulders and watched the waves assail the rocks thirty feet below them. The air was cool, but the sun warmed their skin and the smooth boulders. The water, although clear and cobalt blue, was far too cold for comfortable swimming.

Chanda yawned and rolled onto his stomach. "I could get used to this."

"Don't. I'm already running out of money. We're going to have to decide if we want to stay here or go to Sara's. If we want to stay, then you know what that means."

"Jobs."

"Yeah."

Chanda sat up. "Think about it, man: ten years ago, even five, we couldn't be doing this, traveling across the country, lying on this beach. They'd have run us right back to Soweto."

"Yeah."

"And now, with the elections coming up, who knows?"

Bornwell didn't respond. He rolled onto his stomach and began doing pushups.

"How come every time I bring up the elections, you just go quiet?" Chanda said.

"I don't know. What's to talk about?"

Chanda laughed. "Ah, well, nothing I guess. Just a free South Africa."

"I've been in the bush, man. I don't know anything about politics. I'll leave it all up to you city guys."

"You aren't even going to vote? Think about all the people before us who could never even dream of voting! Man, our parents, they had the pass laws most of their lives, and now we can vote!"

Bornwell scooped up a handful of pebbles from the crevices of the boulders and threw them, one by one, into the ocean. "I didn't say I wasn't going to vote. I just said I'll leave the politics to you city boys."

That afternoon they took a bus to Hertenbosch, one of Cape Town's great old vineyards. The bus discharged them in front of the manicured green lawns that stretched hundreds of feet toward the white Cape Dutch great house that stood with imposing dignity, supported by twin columns flanking outrageously huge cherry-wood doors. They walked slowly toward it, each slightly nervous but determined to keep the other from noticing as much. They paused several times to admire the gardens or scrutinize the expensive cars parked in the shaded gravel lot.

"I'll bet it's still segregated," Chanda said.

"That's illegal."

"Not everywhere. And even where it is, you think it's enforced?"

They hesitated at the open doors, then stepped inside and walked lightly across polished wooden floors. The white walls were covered with ancient portraits and trimmed with elaborate wainscoting. The restaurant and bar were to their left, but they followed the twisting hallway to their right, leading to a sunny outdoor terrace where smartly dressed people, all of them white, enjoyed drinks under forest-green umbrellas.

"Let's have a beer."

"I don't think so, Chanda. I think this is a private club."

This was confirmed seconds later, when a fiercely polite waiter swept them away from the terrace and back to the public bar, where he seated them next to a snooker table. The bar was dark. Bornwell smiled wanly at the white faces that turned to look briefly at them. They sat in silence for a long time before a waiter approached them. When at last one did, it was not to take their order, but to regretfully inform them that they were in violation of the club's dress code. He thanked them for their visit and offered to show them to the door.

"We know the way," Chanda said. He smiled in a way Bornwell had never seen, an eerie, twisted smile of thinly veiled malevolence.

"I am sorry," the waiter said. "Please do return with a coat and tie and we'll be happy to serve you."

Chanda stood but didn't walk. He continued to smile strangely, then stepped toward the waiter and executed a protracted, mocking bow. Bornwell gently pulled on his arm and they walked out.

Outside on the green lawn, Bornwell said, "What the hell was that?"

Chanda dismissively waved his hand back toward the great house. "Fucking rich people. Can you believe that? Coat and tie. I don't see how you could stand it at Umhlaba, all those rich bastards."

Bornwell shrugged. "Some were better than others. And not everyone was rich. It's not that expensive."

"Yeah, I figured you'd say that. Well, whatever, we won't have to deal with attitudes like that much longer." He looked back at the great house, now tinted orange by the slanting rays of the late-afternoon sun. "It's a pretty building," he said. "They call that architecture Cape Dutch, but the Dutch didn't build these places, like they'd have you think. They didn't even design them. You know who did?"

Bornwell shook his head. They reached the bus stop and sat on the iron bench.

"Slaves. Malays, from Portugal. Expert designers and craftsmen. But when it was time to take the credit, the Dutch stepped right up." Chanda shielded his eyes from the sun with his right hand. "You didn't know that?"

"I know the things I need to know."

"Yeah, man. You need to know what a warthog likes for his dinner. And me, and all the other people you look right through every day as you dream of the bush, we need to know when the mine's roof is about to collapse, or when the police aren't bluffing and really mean to shoot . . ." He laughed and patted Bornwell on the arm. "That's it! I just figured it out—you're afraid of the elections because the changes might cost you your chance to be a ranger! You think Mandela is going to turn all the game preserves into farms or something?"

"Ah, it's not that. I just worry there will be chaos and violence, and a lot of changes just for the sake of making changes, but not for the better."

Chanda put his arm around Bornwell's pointy shoulders. "There will be chaos, you know. I can't say it will be for the better, but man, it has to be. Otherwise, people are going to do something about it."

The bus came, and they stood to board it.

"If you never believe another thing I say, man, you better believe this."

36

Bornwell found himself staring at a very pretty young white girl one morning at the waterfront.

Chanda had slept late. Bornwell didn't like waiting at the hostel for him, and, as always, he was uncomfortable with leisure time. He wandered around the waterfront looking for short-term work, found none, but felt better for having tried.

The girl stood at a rack of sunglasses with two others, all of them indiscriminately trying on pairs. Bornwell was fascinated by the grim determination they brought to this task, each of them subjecting their choices to the scrutiny of the others, which in most cases resulted in disapproval. The girl caught Bornwell staring, and for some reason he was incapable of looking away. She smiled at him and left her friends to walk toward him.

"Hey, will you take a picture of me and my friends?" she said.

"Yeah, sure," he said stiffly. He took her small camera and walked with her back to the sunglasses.

"Here we go, let's go, let's go," the girl said, arranging her friends for the picture.

"How does it—where's the button?"

"It's—here, you have to—" the girl broke from her friends and tried to point to the shutter button, but Bornwell suddenly felt like an incompetent child, and he retreated a step.

"I see it, I got it, just—"

"Okay, is it wound? You have to—"

"Yeah, the roller—"

"Just wind it back—"

"It clicked, it's ready, you can—"

"The flash—"

"It's bright enough, we don't need the flash, go ahead and get together," Bornwell said.

"Watch out for your finger," one of the other girls said.

"Shut up, Julie. We're ready."

"Okay," Bornwell said, putting the camera to his face. He had an inspiration. "On three, say 'wildebeest.' That's what we say in the bush."

He counted to three, the girls said "wildebeest," and the camera failed to click.

"It was wound, I heard the click," Bornwell said.

"I think that was actually the shutter. I think you took a picture when you were trying to wind it."

"But you said the roller—"

"It's okay, take another one."

Bornwell felt his face tingling, and one thought raced through his mind: I am fucking this up.

"Okay, ah, one, two, three . . ."

"Wildebeest!"

This time the camera worked to everyone's satisfaction, and Bornwell handed it back with relief.

"Thanks," the girl said. Her friends directed their attention back to the sunglasses. Bornwell smiled back uncertainly, lingered for a moment, then turned to walk away.

"What's the hurry?" the girl said.

"I have to find my cousin. He was still asleep at the hostel." He raised his right arm and pointed in the direction of the hostel, or at least he meant to. He was dimly aware that, unfortunately, he was pointing directly out to sea. The girl laughed, a short, bright burst.

"Well, what's your name? Maybe we'll see you around town."

"Bornwell."

"Okay, Bornwell. I'm Amy. I'll see you." She waved and caught up with her friends, who had moved down the row of shops toward the marina.

He waved back and smiled, feeling he'd somehow been given a reprieve, that although he'd floundered embarrassingly, she hadn't noticed or minded. He turned back toward the hostel and found Chanda standing just a few yards behind him, his arms crossed and the same new, eerie smile on his face.

"Very smooth," he said. "Very, very smooth."

Bornwell started, then composed himself. "When did you get up?"

"One, two, three, wildebeest," Chanda said in a droning monotone, ignoring the question. "That's what we say in the bush."

Bornwell flustered. "Don't be an asshole."

"Really, you should write a book: *How to Get White Women by Being the Village Idiot*."

"Yeah, man, okay. Let's get breakfast."

Mobile food carts and stands lined the walkways along the waterfront. Bornwell and Chanda stood in line at one and bought juice and sugared crepes. As they walked back to the hostel, an old man approached them. He pushed a bicycle laden with paper sacks full of bundled, tattered clothes. Torn sneakers hung by their shoelaces from the rusty frame. He wore layers of rancid clothes.

"I'm trying to get to Durban," the man said to them in Zulu. "But I—"

"You there! Come on, I've told you once!" Bornwell and Chanda turned and saw a policeman walking rapidly toward them from across the street. He was enormously fat, but he moved with a dancer's grace, as if he'd been overweight his entire life and had long ago learned how to comport himself with aesthetic efficiency. "You can't bother people on the street," he said sternly to the old man, placing a hand on his shoulder. "I've told you. Move on now."

"Yes sir, but I wasn't bothering anybody. This man is my cousin!" He pointed at Chanda, who nodded as if he'd expected the man to say that. He felt the policeman's steady gaze swing to him.

"This man is your cousin?" he said.

"He's not bothering us," Chanda said.

"Right, okay. Just get on your way, all of you."

The old man looked at Chanda. "Good-bye, cousin," he said. He started pushing his bicycle and suddenly toppled over when he tried to swing around the policeman. His bicycle clattered to the ground, spilling his pitiful belongings across the sidewalk. Passersby stopped and looked at him as he scrambled to pick up his bags and bundles. A small plastic cartoon fish fell from one of the bags. Chanda picked it up and examined it. It looked back at him with large painted eyes framed by elaborate lashes and a puckered smile. "That's mine," the man whimpered. Chanda handed it to him, and Bornwell helped the man to his feet.

"Ah, now, come on," the policeman said. "Are you okay?"

"He's fine," Chanda said sternly.

"I'm okay," the old man said.

"Go well, cousin," Chanda said to him.

The old man didn't smile, but his eyes widened a bit and he nodded. "Stay well, cousin."

They watched the old man slowly move down the sidewalk. "You, too," the policeman demanded.

"What?" Chanda said.

"You move on, too."

Chanda looked around, as if the policeman were speaking to someone else. "Why?" he said.

"Chanda," Bornwell. "Let's go."

Chanda pointed to a bench in front of a barbershop. "We were going to have a seat. Something wrong with that?"

The policeman's face, which had reflected mild annoyance until then, soured as if he'd just taken a bite from a lemon. He drew himself up to his full height—less impressive than his girth, but still intimidating—and quietly said, "You boys have jobs here?"

"Jobs? No." Chanda said. The policeman waited for further explanation, and Chanda knew this, but he only stared back. The silence between them was charged, the way it is right after someone in a bar says, "What are you looking at?"

Bornwell stepped between them.

37

Bornwell Malaba
c/o Umhlaba Safari Lodge
31 Great Road
Sabie Sands, East Transvaal
Republic of South Africa

Alex Stanzis
225 Key Lime Avenue
Miami, FL 33149

Hey Bornwell,

I hope Umhlaba gets this letter to you. I'm guessing
they have your home address. I just wanted to let
you know that I did make it home, finally, in one
piece. I hate to say it, but I think Chanda set me up
with that driver. The guy took me straight to David
Themba. I know Chanda did it on his own, though,
so I don't blame you or anything. Anyway, it wasn't

such a big deal. That guy David is actually pretty interesting, but some of the others were scary. Stay as far away from them as you can.

Thanks for helping me out and looking after me. One day I'd like to come back and see the bush all over again. Since I lost my camera, I don't have any pictures to show anybody. The same day I got home, there was a nature show on TV that was filmed in Londolozi. That's right near Umhlaba, right? They showed a leopard at night, sitting in a tree. Have you ever seen one like that?

I am back to work here, trying to make up for all that went wrong over there. I have to admit, it was a great adventure though! A few months ago I never would have guessed that I would have been running through Soweto, hiding from a gang of goons. It's kind of flattering actually. Nobody here cares enough about me to chase me down.

I enclosed something for your trouble and efforts. Sorry it couldn't be more—I am still in recovery mode myself. Keep it for yourself—not a penny to Chanda! I hope by now you've found another job. Good luck.

Alex

PS How are the Orlando Pirates doing?

The letter sat on Franz's desk, hidden under government forms and permits, employment applications, bank statements, and accounting papers. He'd picked it up once and read it, but there was nobody left at the lodge who knew where Bornwell had gone.

38

"**D**id I ever tell you about the crocodile made of stars?" Bornwell said.

Chanda, who had been trying to sleep since the lorry driver had picked them up, did not open his eyes. "No." He didn't invite explanation, but Bornwell continued.

"I had a dream one night at Umhlaba. We'd seen a big crocodile that day, on a drive. In my dream it was night, and I was walking in the bush. I went down to the same dam, and the croc was there, only he was made out of stars."

Chanda shifted uncomfortably. "What do you mean?"

"Well, you couldn't see his skin, he was just covered in tiny little white stars, really bright. They were flickering, and he had small spiral galaxies moving around through the stars, too."

Chanda shook his head. "I thought you didn't smoke weed?"

"I don't, stupid, it was just a dream. Anyway, when I saw him I started to run, because I didn't have my gun. But he talked to me." Bornwell paused, but Chanda didn't say anything, so he continued. "He said, 'Where are you going? I won't hurt you.'

"So I said, 'Who are you?' And he said, 'Who do you think? I'm God.' Well, I didn't believe that, and I said so. He said, 'Of course I'm God. In the daytime I carry the sun on my back across the sky. At night I walk alone.' Then he opened his mouth wide, and his teeth were giant and sharp, and they were like diamonds that had colored lights inside them. He coughed, and a cloud of fireflies came out, all blinking. They flew over and landed on me, and I felt this incredible calmness. So then," he said with emphasis, noticing that Chanda had settled back into a sleeping posture, "then this flat dog starts playing a flute—"

"A flute?"

"Yeah, and the animals start coming out of the bush, swaying to the music, and the trees and even the hills are swaying like that, to the little tune he was playing, and it was the most beautiful music I'd ever heard."

"It was just a flute. You don't even like music. You don't even like Lucky Dube."

Bornwell stared out the window at the setting sun. "But it was so pure and clean, that sound. And the notes dropped around me like falling leaves."

Chanda let him sit like that for a moment, then said, "Then what happened?"

Bornwell shrugged. "I woke up. Man, I was so sad when I realized it was just a dream. But the funny part was later that morning, on our drive. We took another group out to the same dam. I told my ranger about the dream on the way out there. When we got there, the same croc was lying on the bank. He must have killed an impala earlier, because there was a big hunk of torn, muddy skin hanging from his mouth, and there were pieces of intestine scattered around him. We drove close to him, and he turned and dove into the dam. His tail sprayed mud and impala guts all over us. You wouldn't believe the stink. 'There's your God,' the ranger said." Bornwell laughed.

Chanda laughed with him. "So God's not really a crocodile."

"Maybe God's a crocodile, he's just not that crocodile."

The lorry droned on through the night. Chanda slept for an hour, then twisted in his seat and woke. "I think I'm catching a cold," he said.

"Don't say it, you'll make it happen."

"Where are we?"

Bornwell peered into the darkness. "I can't tell. I'll ask the oke." He leaned forward into the front of the cab. The driver was about fifty. To Bornwell he looked like most of the Afrikaners he'd known—ruddy skin, thick beard and mustache, reddish-brown hair that leapt in all directions at once from his head, sun-crinkled face with a network of tiny broken capillaries crisscrossing his bulbous nose. He'd heard somewhere that Afrikaners have one of the highest rates of heart disease in the world. He believed it. The Afrikaner rangers he knew ate nothing but animal fat, steaks and pork loins and ribs, night after night, and bread drenched in butter, and salads cloaked in creamy dressings. And they drank. The rangers went through several cases of beer every week. One week they ran out, and the grocery van was a day late. They cursed and bitched and refused to work until one of the camp boys was dispatched to Nelspruit for an emergency supply.

Bornwell rarely drank, and though he knew he ate too much red meat when he was in the bush, he at least made sure to eat fresh vegetables every day, and he didn't drown his bread in butter. He had an oddly intense intolerance for overweight people, probably in deference to all those who he knew went hungry back home.

The driver said, "Oh, you awake now?"

"Yeah, where are we?"

"Ag, who knows, probably getting near Durban. Long way to go still. Have a seat."

Bornwell sat in the passenger seat. He surveyed the array of backlit dials and knobs on the dashboard. "There's a lot to keep you busy," he said.

"I don't worry about most of it. Oil pressure and water temperature are the only important ones. Well, and fuel." He pulled a cigarette from his shirt pocket. "Can't remember if we did names or not. You boys went right to sleep. I'm Jan."

"I'm Bornwell. He's Chanda."

"He's the sleepy one, eh?"

"He's a professional sleeper. You'll see, he won't wake until we're there."

They came to a small village where the speed limit made it feel as if they were walking. There was a *shebeen*[1] at the only intersection. Bornwell could see inside as they drove past. One bare lightbulb hung from a wire, and under it, a dozen people danced happily to music he couldn't hear. Probably township jive, or reggae by Lucky Dube.

"That's it," Jan said as they pulled away from the town. "That's all there is to see for the next few hours. I just about go mad every time I make this run. Nothing to look at all day and night."

Jan then narrated the complete history of his life, how he'd been one of the youngest supervisors in the gold mines until he was fired for coming to work drunk—"It was the day after the Springboks beat the All Blacks, you understand"—and a friend got him into the lorry-driving business. "When I first started, I was doing the Joburg-Windhoek run. I was living in a little house in the northern suburbs—not the nice part, like it all is today. We were in the middle of nowhere. It was me and Lucy, my wife, and her brother came to stay with us because he broke his arm in a fight—he told Lucy it was a car accident, but he told me it was a fight—and he'd lost his job. Every day when I got home he would just be lying there on my couch, drinking my Castle, and his friends used to come over at night to keep him company . . ." He trailed away into silence, then after a moment said, "Where did you say you boys need to go?"

"Bosbokrand, right next to the Kruger. So what happened?"

"What happened when?"

---

[1] *Shebeen*—beer hall.

"With the fellow, your brother-in-law."

"Ag, that. I forget the rest of it. It doesn't matter anyway. He's gone, Lucy's gone. I got a new girl now." He smiled and lovingly patted the dashboard. "She takes all my time."

Outside, the lorry's headlight pushed back the darkness in two cones, and the wind blew hard from the west, across Umfolozi and Hluhluwe and the wild tangles of Natal, and in the cab, Jan braced his shoulders and said, "Nothing to look at, nothing to see." He'd picked up two hitchhikers, and one was asleep and the other wasn't very talkative, and, as far as he knew, they could be criminals on the run, but the road was long and empty, and he was glad for the company.

39

As Bornwell and Chanda crossed the country, Franz struggled to keep control of his lodge. The coming elections divided his staff along clear and increasingly hostile lines. The lodge reopened to guests after the midsummer shutdown, and although most of his staff came from the rural, politically apathetic towns of the Eastern Transvaal, the extensive media coverage of the elections fanned curiosity into passion among his multitribal staff.

Franz wasn't concerned about his three guides. All of them were mature men in their fifties, who had spent almost all of their lives in the bush. Two were from Mozambique and had no real stake in the elections anyway. It was the kitchen staff and grounds crew, mostly teenage boys, who reveled in the impending moment of history. Most of the boys were ANC supporters, but a few were Inkatha, and angry words between them threatened to escalate into something more violent. Some of their arguments had been seen and heard by guests in the intimate camp.

One evening, Franz brought all the employees together and explained that if they couldn't work out their differences peacefully and privately, he would sack the lot of them. His word was respected for a few days, but emotions ran high and tempers proved irrepressible. Franz had to fire two dishwashers who exchanged punches in the middle of the dinnertime rush. Fortunately, none of the guests saw the fight, but Franz knew the camp would be crackling with tension for weeks. Even after the elections there were bound to be hard feelings.

Pollen Ndlanya, Franz's longtime cook, drove the terminated dishwashers to Nelspruit and dropped them off in the middle of town. When he returned, he went to Franz's office.

"I'm back. It's done."

"Thanks, Pollen."

"I got you some cigarettes, too."

"Ag, man! I'm trying to quit!"

"But you told Hennie this morning you wanted cigarettes."

"I just meant I wish I *could* smoke, not that I wanted to. Ag, forget it. Give them to me."

Pollen handed the carton to Franz. "This is bound to happen again."

"No, no. No matter what I say later, don't ever buy them for me again."

"Not the cigarettes. The fighting."

Franz leaned back in his chair and scanned Pollen's face. "Why do you say that?"

Pollen shrugged. "There's no hiding from it. Even in the bush."

"Ya, I know."

The two men stood looking at each other. Pollen smiled wanly. "I've got to get back." He walked to the door, then paused. "Do you want to know what I think is going to happen?"

"Happen when?" Franz said.

"After the elections."

"Ya, what?"

"Mandela will win," Pollen said.

"I know that," Franz said, laughing. "But what then?"

Pollen tilted his head at Franz's rock posters. In a distracted manner he said, "Some of the staff might quit, thinking maybe there's better jobs for them in the cities."

"That's all?"

"Here, yes. That's all. Everywhere else, I can't say. Except that maybe it will look good on the news, but won't really be so good."

Franz sat forward. "I hope it is good. I hope things do get better. Not all us Dutchies supported everything about apartheid. I'd almost vote for Mandela myself, you know. He seems like a good man. But F.W. has proved he can change with the times, and he has the experience of being a president."

Pollen shrugged. "We don't have to agree. You don't have to try to convince me of anything."

Franz nodded. He rose from his desk. "I'll go with you. I've got to get lunch."

They walked across the lodge together. It was cloudy for once, and Pollen said, "It might actually rain, God forbid!"

"Ya, imagine that?" Franz kicked at the dry ground, scattering pebbles and dust.

"My father was a farmer, you know," Pollen said. "He used to say rain was a present from God, and when there wasn't rain, God was punishing him."

Franz ran a finger across a camelthorn leaf and showed the dust to Pollen. "God has been punishing me for five years. What did your father do to make God happy again, so it would rain?"

"Nothing. He wasn't a very good Christian. He had hoses."

Sara met them in front of the post office in Bosbokrand, where Jan dropped them off just after sunrise. Bornwell introduced Chanda to Sara, and she said, "I know about you."

"Oh yeah? What do you know?"

"Bornwell told me stories. I don't know whether to believe him or not," she said. She was only joking, but Bornwell panicked and said, "I didn't say anything bad!"

Chanda laughed. "It's all true, I'm sure. But I'm better now."

They drove to Sara's house in her car, an old, dusty Honda. After the initial friendliness, a tense silence descended on the car. Sara and Bornwell didn't know each other very well, and Chanda and Sara didn't know each other at all. From the cramped rear seat, he snuck looks at her as she drove. She was short and thin—too thin, he thought, like she was sick—and wore her hair in an unflattering, ironed-straight style. Her face was oval, a shape accentuated by her skinny neck and angular shoulders, and her skin was much lighter than his own. He thought her eyes were pretty, but the furrowed brow above them gave her a joyless air.

"That's the community center," she said, pointing out a new wooden building standing in an open space along the road. "We built it in October."

"What do you do there?" Chanda said.

She frowned. "Just a few classes for the children. We have to raise more money for instructors and supplies before we can do more."

"It sounds nice," Bornwell said.

"Yeah, you remember the center in Izolo?" Chanda said to Bornwell. "It sounds like the same kind of thing. Remember, they wanted to teach us to cook and make things from wood, but we just wanted to hide and play in the drapes?"

"This isn't the same thing," Sara said. "It's not a daycare center. It's an educational center."

Chanda nodded and smiled obligingly. "Right, right. How long have you worked there?"

Sara suddenly accelerated around a man riding a rickety bicycle in the middle of the street. She tooted her horn at him and waved her fist, but she was smiling, and he smiled and waved back at her. "That's Jerry. He's the social services district supervisor here. The first black one they've had."

"So how long—"

"I just volunteer there. I still work full-time at the lodge."

"How is everything there?" Bornwell asked, trying to sound casual.

Sara shrugged. "Not bad. You should ask after Hennie though. He's been ill. Something with his stomach."

They pulled up to her house, a small, charmless square cottage raised on cinderblocks.

"Nice place," Chanda said as they walked to the door.

Sara paused at the front step. "I've never had visitors," she said. "I don't have time for cleaning." She pointed at an old tire lying half underneath the raised house. Weeds sprouted from its center. "That's been there since before I moved in."

David Themba walked to the Barcelona shebeen and bought a small bag of weed from one of the flunky regulars there. He got his bag and walked back to the Mandelaville shanty, one of many places he'd been sleeping. He felt it was smart to keep moving. Often he didn't sleep at all, remaining alert and guarded throughout the night, taking his sleep in short spells during the relative safety of daylight. It was no way to live, and he knew it. But it was temporary.

A warm, jabbing wind came from the dry west. He smelled the cooking fires inside shanties and the garbage in the street. Like the residents of river towns, who seem not to mind or notice the rank odor of dark water, David rarely noticed these smells. But tonight they were vivid. They swirled and mixed with the hums and murmurs, dog barks and occasional shouts and howls of laughter, and formed a gray, neutral aroma of resignation along the sticky, red street. It never rained, and there was little good water in Mandelaville, but the streets always seemed to be running and muddy. He wondered how that could be—spit, sweat, piss, blood? The shanties careened in front of him on the swell of a moping grade. He was sweating. The wind came again and cooled his face. He drew the back of his hand across his brow, and the sweat dropped in two tiny pats into the ochre mud. It was very dark. He shook his head to clear his vision, which had been going blurry for the last hour. Snakes wrestled in his stomach, and his throat tightened as the awful and familiar clutches of nausea began washing over him. It was going to be a sick night, he knew, and he smiled grimly at the prospect. He was getting sick like this once or twice a week now. The weed would help.

Two shadows rose in front of him, then a third. Three men. They stood in his path and waited for him, but he walked by without looking at their faces. They let him walk several feet before one called to him.

"David Themba?"

"What the fuck do you want?" David said flatly, continuing to walk. They turned and caught up to him, and this time they closed tightly around him. But he continued walking, and no one tried to stop him. "I'm not stopping," David said calmly.

"You'll stop." One of the men put out his right hand and pressed it against David's chest. "Do you remember me?"

David gently removed the man's hand and squinted at him. "No."

"I'm Mark Milliken. My brother is called Carlton. You remember Carlton Milliken?"

David did. Carlton was a dim boy who tried to impress him by beating up smaller boys and stealing from shops. David snubbed him, so Carlton smeared childish graffiti about Kusasa on several walls. Steve caught him and brought him to David, who casually punched Carlton around and told him to stay out of Izolo.

"Yeah, I remember Carlton. I was easy on him. I could have beaten him a lot worse, and I will, if he fucks with me again."

Mark Milliken suddenly struck a formal boxing pose.

"No you won't. You're going to fight me instead. Then we'll see who gets a beating, motherfucker!"

David laughed. "Three against one," he said, pointing to the others. "Pretty good odds for you."

"They won't do anything, they just came to see for themselves. So let's go!" Mark bounced from foot to foot, like a trained boxer, with his fists raised high in front of his face. He was an inch taller than David and at least twenty pounds heavier. Even in the dim light David could see his knuckles were scarred. He'd been in a lot of fights. David also saw that he was a left-hander.

David put his bag of weed in his back pocket and stepped toward Mark. He calmly ducked the first wild punch and shot his left foot out, kicking Mark hard in his left knee. The knee buckled and crunched. The bigger man howled in pain and lurched forward, trying to keep his weight off his left leg. David cocked his right fist behind his ear and snapped three quick jabs to Mark's head. The first two caught him square in the mouth, the third on the jaw, and he flinched in pain and tried to cover his face as David snapped more punches at him. He grabbed Mark by the arms and said, "This can stop now, if you say so. Or it can get a lot worse."

Mark's breath was ragged. He spat blood. "I'm not hurt," he said, and yanked his right arm free. He lashed out with both fists and did land a short punch to David's cheek, but he was already tired, and his punches soon plodded harmlessly. It was over quickly when David cracked another short right cleanly to Mark's temple, dropping him to the ground. He gazed up at David with a nonplussed expression. His friends helped him to his feet. His cut lips were badly swollen.

"This is the last fucking thing I needed tonight," David groused. "You better keep your eyes open from now on. Anybody sees you in Izolo, they're shooting."

"Wait a minute," Mark said thickly through his bleeding mouth. He looked at his friends, and the three men decided something with the look. "We want to join you," Mark said, wincing as he spoke.

"Join me . . . join me," David said flatly. He smiled, but it was an empty, joyless smile. "This is how you tell me, by jumping me?"

"But we had to see if you were strong. Some people say . . ."

"Say what?"

Mark hesitated. "They say, maybe you have other people to do your fighting for you. That's not a man to follow."

David nodded. "And now you see it isn't like that."

"Yes. We've thought about it a lot."

David rubbed his sore knuckles. "I've got enough muscle with me already," he said.

"We aren't goons!" Mark protested. "I just finished my political science degree at Wits! These two are students there still."

David shrugged. "We'll see. I'll have to know I can trust you. That'll take some time. I'll send someone to talk to you."

Mark nodded eagerly. "We want to join you," he said again, emphatically. David smiled in spite of himself. He turned and walked into the dark.

"Where will we meet the man you send?" Mark called.

"Come to the Barcelona tomorrow, early. I'll send someone."

When he got back to the shanty, he sat in the center of the floor and rolled a small joint with shaky hands. He hadn't eaten much that day, and, after the exertion of the fight, felt dizzy and weak. Some of the others were there, sitting quietly in the corners, watching David, trying to make conversation. He ignored them and smoked the joint until it was reduced to a tiny, glowing sliver, then braced his head against a wall and waited like that through the hot night, waited for the spinning to cease and the sickness to stop or just carry him away.

42

"Explain this to me again," Sara said. She poured herself another glass of wine and offered more to Chanda and Bornwell, but neither had yet finished his first glass. "You brought this American to David, like he wanted, but . . . he's still mad at you?"

"Yes, I think so. He wouldn't even see me when I went to smooth things over," Chanda said.

"And his goon Steve attacked us," Bornwell added.

"Ah, Steve hates my guts anyway. I'd really like to know why David wouldn't talk to me, but not getting killed by Steve was my top priority at the moment."

Bornwell nodded. "He said he was going to get us."

"So you ran. All the way to Cape Town."

Chanda smiled and spread his arms. "You'd have to see Steve. He's fucking huge!"

"Won't he be just as big when you get home?"

"Yeah, but he's dumb. He'll have forgotten about us."

"I see," Sara said. "Yes. A foolproof plan."

Chanda said, "You're making it sound stupider than it is. We just used it as an excuse to do some sightseeing."

"Well, who's David, then? Is he a thug? He sounds like it." She shook her head. "The boys around here, they don't have any role models at all. Their fathers work in Joburg, or in the mines. We have a few thugs like David here, and the boys think they're important, so they all want to be like them."

"David's not a thug," Chanda said.

"Come on. He is," Bornwell said.

Chanda shook his head. "No. Really, he's not a thug. He's a smart fellow. You've never talked to him, Bornwell. You wouldn't know."

"But he is a criminal," Sara said.

"Yeah, I guess so." For reasons he didn't understand, Chanda felt the need to defend David. Perhaps it was because Sara didn't know what she was talking about, going on as she had all night about the "tragedies of the townships" and how community centers like hers were going to solve all the problems of black South Africans. It might work out here, he thought, in a small burg with no gangs, but in Mandelaville?

"David's an honest guy. He just has a lot of thugs who follow him," he said, then paused, wondering where to go from there. "See, what you don't know—and you really don't either, Bornwell—is what life is like in Izolo, and places like it. You take your community center there, and maybe for a while the kids will play there and learn things. But eventually people are going to steal your toys and books, because they don't have any of their own, and at night people will break in and sleep there, and before you know it, it's not your community center anymore."

"That's silly," Sara said. "People will see that it's a place for them, to make their lives better."

"In the long run, maybe. But there're too many desperate people there who won't feel like waiting around. If they can steal your drapes, or your gas heater, or your pots, they will."

Sara shook her head. "It hasn't been like that here. The people here—"

"The people here aren't like us!" Chanda said, a little too

firmly. "Yeah, look around. They have fresh running water. They have a school with no police out front. They can walk home without getting stopped by gangs. There're no she-beens here with fifty drunks spilling out all day and night. You think this is a township? This is just a few huts and houses and some barbed wire. You want a township, come on home with me."

Sara stared back at him. Bornwell coughed and said, "Well, Chanda, it's not really fair, is it? You and me, we don't live in Mandelaville, either. We can at least get water—"

"But we only have to walk around the corner to see people who don't," Chanda said.

Sara finished her glass of wine. "I never said this was Soweto," she said quietly. Chanda heard the hurt in her voice and instantly regretted his aggressiveness. "But human nature is human nature, here just like where you live. If I had the chance, I'd prove it." She shrugged. "But I'm here. It's small, but we're helping people. I'm sorry if that bothers you."

"Why don't we—"

"Shut up, Bornwell," Chanda said, flaring up again. "Look, nothing you're doing here bothers me. But you shouldn't think township problems are so simple that a community center in the middle of nowhere can solve them."

"I know that. But I'm just one person. What more do you want me to do? Community centers help, so I work at a community center. Volunteer, actually," she said. "What do you do to make things better?"

Chanda leaned back and fingered his wine glass. He smiled to himself. "I don't do anything for the cause. I'm trying to fix things one person at a time."

"Starting with you," she said flatly.

He nodded. "Starting with me."

43

The bush was so close. At night, sleeping on a cot in Sara's living room, Bornwell thought he could smell it—the itchy dustiness, the raw, rank rivers, the rich, fertile scent of dung—and after a few days he could stand it no longer. He convinced Chanda to accompany him to a remote stretch of wild bush land in the Timbavati, a private game preserve. Bornwell knew the chief ranger of the area, and after one phone call, they had a pass to stay in a rangers' camp near the Ulatella River. "It's been out of use for months," the ranger warned. "There might be nothing left but four poles and a wood floor. Bring plenty of food with you."

The visit lasted just three days. While they did have plenty of food, their water ran low almost immediately. Bornwell had been counting on the river, but they found it nearly dry. He managed to scrape up a few canteens of silty dribblings, which they boiled over a fire, but it was far too muddy and salty to drink. Chanda also quickly proved to be a liability. After his initial enthusiasm, which peaked when Bornwell led him to a pair of grazing white rhinos, he began complaining about the daytime heat, the nighttime cold, the dust, and the flimsy, cramped hut. He also constantly worried about the low fence that surrounded the camp, believing it incapable of protecting them from the lions they heard roaring at night. Bornwell's nerves began to fray. Had he been alone, he thought, he could have stayed at least a month, despite the water shortage.

On their last night at the camp, Bornwell woke after sleeping deeply for a few hours. He stretched and yawned in the little hut, felt for his shoes in the darkness, and crept outside. Chanda stirred but did not wake. Bornwell visited the rangers' old outhouse. It wasn't especially cold, though he could see his breath in a little cloud in front of his face. When he finished in the outhouse, he sat on a large *koppie*[1] near the hut and rolled his head, trying to loosen the knots that had accumulated from sleeping on the bumpy cot. He was completely awake now. He watched the sky for satellites, but a heavy nocturnal mist settled overhead, obscuring all but the brightest stars.

He leaned against the cool rocks and waited patiently for sleep to come again. On previous nights, he had heard wildebeest shuffling in the darkness, the sound of their scuffling hooves and plaintive grunts and coughs carrying several miles to his attuned ears. Tonight he heard nothing, but after several minutes a tiny pebble suddenly cascaded down from the top of the koppie and bounced off his left knee on the way to the ground. Bornwell recognized the earthy scent of a wild animal and was mildly surprised that one would venture so near their camp. He slid silently off the rock and stepped back. Looking up, he found himself staring into the face of a spotted hyena, thirty feet above and behind him. The silhouette of the ungainly animal stood in sharp relief against the creamy sky. It had evidently just noticed Bornwell, for it froze suddenly and remained statuesque as Bornwell gently crept back into the hut. He knew

---

[1] *Koppie* — small rock hill in the bush veld.

better than to stand around at night with a hyena in close quarters.

Bornwell considered waking Chanda, but the hyena quickly disappeared behind the koppie. Moments later he heard it drop to the ground and shuffle into the dry darkness. He lay with his head out of the hut for a long time, searching the faint outlines of nearby rocks and hills to see if the animal would reappear there. This is how the morning sun found him, and when he was awakened by its warm rays, he wondered if he'd simply dreamt it.

The short stay had not satisfied Bornwell's longing for the bush. Indeed, he now found himself unable to concentrate on anything else—certainly not Chanda and Sara's boring political arguments. He called Franz and asked if it would be okay for him to visit Umhlaba again, and Franz invited him to come that very day and stay for dinner.

He rode in with Sara, and after seeing her into the restaurant, he walked to Franz's office. The grounds looked different, somehow smaller, now that he'd crossed the plains, plateaus, and deserts of his country. Smaller, but he felt he was home again.

Hennie saw him, shook his hand, and asked how he was, all in a manner that struck Bornwell as automated, distracted. They talked for a minute, and the ranger told him Franz was on a game drive. "He takes two drives a day now, the boss does. He has to. There's only four of us now."

"Only four? What—"

"Had to let more people go. It's not so good here anymore."

"Sara told me you've been sick."

"Yeah," Hennie sighed. "Nothing so serious. Just ulcers."

"I'm sorry to hear it."

"It was good news, man. At first they thought it could be cancer. They never said that word, but I knew that's what they were worried about from the tests they did." He shook his head. "I thought I was going to have to give this up—move back to the city. What a nightmare."

Bornwell forced a smile.

"Oh, cuzzie! I didn't mean — damn, I forgot. I know you didn't want to leave —"

"It's okay," Bornwell assured him. "But you're right. It's been a nightmare. Don't ever leave."

"Not if I can help it."

Hennie told him Franz would be back at three, so Bornwell went for a short walk through the bush around camp. Then he walked down the little path that he had trampled flat, through the crackly scrub, to his own little hut. Looking through the window, he found the small structure filled with boxes of paperwork and supplies. It was an obvious fire hazard, and he was surprised Franz allowed it.

He tried the door but it was locked. He lingered outside for a few minutes, sat for a while under the tree where often he'd eaten his meals and studied his books. There was still a matted area where the growth of the thin grass had been stunted by his persistent sitting.

At three o'clock he took a seat outside Franz's office and waited. The big man didn't return until almost four. He was happy to see Bornwell, but he, too, seemed distracted.

"I'm surprised I haven't heard from you more," Franz said, sifting through mail on his desk. "Got something for you here." He handed Bornwell the letter from Alex Stanzis. "What have you been doing?"

Bornwell told him of the problems with Kusasa, of traveling with Chanda. Then they talked about the lodge, which, Bornwell quickly saw, was upsetting Franz.

"You're better off, believe it or not," Franz said. He laughed bitterly. "Before it's over, I'll be the head ranger, head waiter, and cook."

"Have you heard anything about . . ."

"Nothing since we last talked. I still expect to hear from Peter van Himst at Sabi Sabi."

"I still wish I was coming back here," Bornwell said.

"No you don't."

Franz invited Bornwell to stay for dinner, and as night fell, they ate at the boma around a raging fire. Despite the tensions among the staff, and Franz's depression, it was a happy night. The rangers ate and drank and laughed, and there was no edge to it, and the guests were happy to bask in the glow the rangers radiated at times like these.

Sara came from the kitchen and said it was time to leave. Franz saw Bornwell was reluctant, and offered to drive him back the next morning if he wanted to stay the night. Bornwell declined. He knew Franz had enough to do in the morning without adding a round trip to Bosbokrand.

He wasn't good company on the ride home. Leaving Umhlaba on this night was no easier than it had been weeks before. "Was it like you remembered?" Sara asked as they jostled along the dirt road.

"Mostly. It's smaller now."

"Did you go to your old hut?"

Bornwell smiled ruefully and held his hands as high as the car would allow. "I've been replaced," he said grandly, "by boxes."

"**O**f course you don't feel well," Sara was saying to Chanda when Bornwell entered the kitchen the next morning. "All you eat is meat. You're filled with toxins."

Chanda smiled back at her. "Toxins," he said. "What are those?"

"Toxins—you know, pollutants."

"So there are pollutants in the meat we eat, but not in anything you eat?"

"Not as much," she said.

"Vegetarian," he said to himself. Chanda looked at Bornwell and smiled his eerie smile. Bornwell could see he was baiting Sara, looking for another argument. "And these toxins, they go from the meat to my body, and they make me feel bad?"

"That's right."

"So it's the toxins in my food, and not the eleven Castles I drank last night, that's giving me this headache."

Sara slapped him playfully on the arm. "I didn't know

you drank last night! You were already asleep when we got home. Bastard, here I was, actually worrying about you."

They noticed Bornwell. "So how was it last night? Trip down memory lane?" Chanda said to him.

"It was nice. Really nice." Bornwell sat down with them.

"You seemed depressed about it last night," Sara said.

"Yes, but now, I guess, I'm happy just to be close enough to visit anytime."

Chanda looked up at him in alarm. "What do you mean by 'anytime'? I thought we were heading back home this week?"

Bornwell scratched his head and grimaced. "About that . . ."

"Steve's probably in jail or dead by now anyway," Chanda said wistfully.

"Probably."

"So then, let's go. You can't stay here. What are you going to do? We've got to give Sara her house back." Sara started to object, but Chanda stopped her. "You know it's true. Sooner or later. We have to go home."

Bornwell fidgeted. "It's not about Steve or David," he said. "I just don't want to leave." Chanda stared at him blankly. "It's so close," Bornwell said, raising his hands and then dropping them into his lap in frustration. He gestured out the window, toward the bush. "The closer I stay, the better chance I have to get another job here."

Chanda shook his head, then coughed raggedly. "God, my head. I think I'm getting sick. Hot during the day, cold at night. It always gets me."

They were all silent for a moment. Then Sara said, "You can stay, but the vacation is over. I need help."

"At the restaurant?" he said with hope.

"No, at the center. I'll tell you what: we can put on classes for the kids. You can teach them about the bush. Most of these kids here, they live ten miles from Kruger but they've never seen an elephant in their lives. Show them some pictures, or slides, something like that."

"They can follow in your footsteps," Chanda said to Bornwell. "You can save them from a life of poverty with pictures of hyena shit."

Bornwell smiled and shot Chanda a discreet obscene ges-
ture. He turned to see if Sara had noticed, and saw her
walking to the open front door. Four small faces peered in
at them. "We have company," Sara said.

The four tiny children looked frightened and refused to
enter until Sara took the closest one by the hand and led
him inside. "This is George," she said. "And that's his sister Mynah. And this here," she said, pointing to a boy with
a bulbous stomach and tight, orange-tinted hair, "this is
Rogers, my best finger-painter. And this is Elizabeth, who
just turned seven." Sara walked to the table and stood
behind Bornwell and Chanda. "These are my friends," she
said to the kids. "This is Bornwell—he'll be teaching you at
the center soon—and this is Chanda."

Tiny Rogers said, "We came like you told us."

"I see! I'm so proud of you. George, why don't you take
everyone down to the bathroom and I'll be right there. You
can all sit together in the tub, but don't run any water."

"Do we have to get shots again?"

"No, not this time. I told you, it won't be so bad this time.
Go on ahead."

The children shuffled down the short hall and entered
the bathroom. Sara turned to Bornwell and Chanda. "Why
don't you take a walk into town. Get something to cook for
dinner. I think they'll be more comfortable if you aren't
here."

"What are you doing with them?" Bornwell said.

Sara lowered her voice. "I volunteer a couple of days
every month at Retief Hospital, in exchange for whatever
extra supplies they can spare." She picked up a small bottle
from the counter next to the refrigerator. "They gave me
this last time. Lice solution."

Bornwell nodded. "Yeah, we'll go to town."

"Give me an hour," Sara said.

They walked outside and down the road in silence, until
Chanda said, "That's pretty decent of her."

"It is. I told you she was like that, but you made fun of
her."

Chanda shook his head. "I thought she was just all talk."

"No, she really wants to do good."

"You should do that, at the center. Teach them about the bush, I mean. Show some pictures, tell them those stories you've told me."

Bornwell nodded. "You could stay and help, too."

"No, I'm going to go sometime this week. I need to go home."

They shopped for dinner in the small market and passed the rest of the hour in front of the center, talking to the old man Jerry, the social services director.

Back at Sara's house, they found her sitting alone and grim.

"Where are the kids?" Bornwell asked.

"We finished. I sent them home." She stood and paced, then sat back down. "Chanda, you got a message. You— I'm not sure how they knew you were here, but . . ." She stood. "Can you wait out front, Bornwell? I'm expecting another group of kids. If they come, can you just send them home and tell them to come back at the same time tomorrow?"

"No problem." He met Chanda's eyes. "What the hell, man? You think Steve or David tracked us down here?"

"No way. I don't know what's up, but I'll find out."

Bornwell waited on the front step. Ten minutes later, Chanda opened the door. "I have to go now," he said. Bornwell saw he was crying, and came inside.

"What's going on?"

"My father is dead. There was an accident in the mine." He gathered his clothes and stuffed them into his bag. "They don't know what happened. Probably a collapse, or gas. Same old fucking things."

"Jesus Christ, man," Bornwell murmured. "I'm really sorry."

"Chanda," Sara said softly. "There's not even a bus until this evening. Why don't you sit."

"I don't care. I'm going back now. I'll hitch. I'll fucking walk."

"I could just drive you back, then."

"No, you can't. You're busy here. And it wouldn't be fair,

your car is too old. No." He sat down heavily. "I'll just wait for the bus."

Bornwell sat next to him. "Who called? Your mother?"

"Yeah. She called your mother, your mother called Franz, Franz called here."

Sara went into the kitchen and returned with a pair of Castle Lagers. "There's only two left."

That evening, Bornwell and Sara drove him to the bus station, and when his bus was about to depart, Chanda took Bornwell's hand. "It's been fun," he said. "Thanks for showing me the country."

"You'll be okay at home?"

Chanda shrugged. "I don't think David would ever let Steve hurt me. I'll just have to stay away from that psycho." Then he hugged Sara. "I didn't mean anything by teasing you," he said. "I think it's good what you're doing here."

She smiled sadly. "Thank you. I think you'll do good, too."

"In my own time, in my own way," he said. He looked at Bornwell. "You know, David was right."

"About what?"

"About the mines."

He climbed aboard and sat down at the window seat closest to where Sara and Bornwell stood. The bus quickly filled, and people crowded into the aisle, grasping the rings that hung from the ceiling. They waited while the driver had a cup of coffee at the lunch counter in the station. Chanda pushed down the window and stuck his head outside, and the three of them chatted until the driver returned and the diesel engine belched to life.

"Hm, the two of you, alone in that little house," Chanda said, as the driver released the air brakes. He smiled at Bornwell. "Don't even think it, cousin. I can tell she doesn't go for dark-skinned men." Bornwell flushed furiously. "But you look good together, you two. Don't go doing anything I wouldn't do!"

Bornwell felt Sara looking at him, but he couldn't face

her. He waved to Chanda as the bus pulled away. "I don't know where he got that idea," he said defensively.

"Relax, Bornwell. I'm safer with you than with any fellow I know."

"That's right." He dared to glance at her and saw she was not teasing him. "Well, I mean . . . but yeah, you are. Chanda likes to try to be funny."

"I know." They walked back to her car. "I tell you, I don't like to think what's going to happen to him."

"Chanda? He'll be okay. He always finds a way to get by."

"But that was before David," she reminded him.

Bornwell cocked his head. "You didn't believe him when he said David wouldn't hurt him?"

She laughed softly. "Don't you wonder how he seems to know David won't hurt him? Didn't you hear the way he defended the guy that night? And what he just said, about David being right about the mines?"

"So what?"

"So there's something to it. It sounds like David got his hook in Chanda a long time ago." She started the car and clicked on the radio. "Sooner or later he's going to reel him in."

David Themba stood over Chanda in the burnt-out hulk of an old shanty in Jabavu, Soweto, and said, "What do you remember about the '76 riots?"

Chanda shifted in his chair. "It was because of Afrikaans. We didn't want them teaching in Afrikaans anymore."

"You say 'we.' How did you personally feel about it?"

Chanda did some quick math in his head. "David, I was just six years old."

David nodded. "Okay, sure. So, what do you remember?"

"Well, I went to school as usual, and we all marched toward Phefeni . . ." his voice trailed away.

"And that's when you ran," David finished.

"When I saw the police. But not because I was afraid!"

"Why, then?"

"Because of my mother."

David stopped his slow circumnavigation of Chanda. He placed both hands over his face, as if he were shielding himself from the sun, and spoke through his fingers. "What did your mother have to do with the riots?"

"Not so much my mother, but Alton, my older brother. He—"

"Alton," David said. "I remember. Shot by the police the year before."

"Alton didn't do anything wrong," Chanda said. "He didn't know the boys he was with were going to rob the store."

"So, when you saw the police, you thought of what happened to Alton, and what it did to your mother . . ."

"Right. So I ran."

David smiled tightly. "Smart, smart." He knelt down and grasped the arms of Chanda's chair. "Do you remember Stephen, my older brother?"

Chanda nodded. "I never knew him. We were all afraid of him. But I remember him."

David stood. He spoke without looking at Chanda, louder, for the benefit of the shadows lounging quietly in the corners of the shanty. "Stephen was in high school during the riots. He was one of the student leaders. A month after the first rioting, he was arrested in Alexandra. They beat him in prison. When he came out he wasn't the same . . ."

The air was still and hot in the little room. Chanda cleared his throat and fidgeted.

"Wasn't the same. He lost interest in the cause, in politics. He doesn't care at all anymore."

David shook his head sadly. "Smart, man. It was smart of you to run that day," he said. "There's a time to stand and fight, but there's a time to cut your losses and run, too. But those fighting times—can you recognize those? Would you stand and fight then, if you had to?"

"I can recognize them. But I can avoid them from the start, too."

"Not here, not anymore. If you stay in Izolo, those situations will be unavoidable, whether or not you work with me. You'll see those days again, just like '76. You'll be a victim. You won't have any say in your own life." He stepped close to Chanda. "But if you work with me, you can take action, steps toward a better life for yourself, and for everyone in Soweto."

"If that is really your goal," Chanda said, garnering courage, "then why do you terrorize people? Why do you use violence against the people you say you want to help? Me and Bornwell had to run all over the country because we were afraid your goon Steve was going to kill us."

David laughed. "That had nothing to do with me. You pissed Steve off somehow. I can't keep him on a leash. And Bornwell"—he waved a hand in derision—"the hell with him. He wants to be a ranger, let him be a ranger. But this violence question is just what you can help me with. See, back when I started, when I began organizing a political movement, we were still under all the old laws. None of my classmates at Wits University, nobody with any education or intelligence or anything to lose, none of them would join with me. The risk was too great. Imprisonment without trial, beatings, exile. The only people who would follow me were people with nothing to lose—young punks, thugs, criminals. I recruited some of them from MK. How was I to know? They were useful at first, but they got a taste of power, and it wasn't long before they started overdoing it. And it's true, I let it happen, I was enjoying the power, too, back then. Plus, that was when I found out I was sick. I don't like to talk about it," he said, holding up a hand. "I've come to terms with it now. But when I first found out I had it, it made me even more careless. Now I'm saddled with these people, and it's true, we deserve our bad reputation. But I want that to change, and that's why I want people like you. People I can trust to make sound decisions."

Chanda didn't say anything.

"Look, if all I wanted to do was continue with thuggery, why would I want you to join me? You're no fighter. We both know that."

Chanda nodded. "The sickness . . . aren't there treatments for it?"

David shook his head. "Too expensive. They don't work anyway."

"I still don't see how I could help you . . ."

"You can help me by being realistic. These fellows," he swept an arm around the room. "Burn this! Break that!

Shoot everybody! That's how revolutions end, not begin. Remember what we're up against: Mandela, de Klerk, Buthelezi, Ramaphosa, Terreblanche. None of them have township interests at heart. They've made deals with each other, with the Americans, the Communists left in Russia, deals we know nothing about."

"Even Mandela?"

"Of course even Mandela. How do you think he got off of Robbins Island? And the ANC is to blame for splitting the black nation into fragments. Do you remember how the hostel workers from Mzimhilope turned against the students in '76, attacking children? It was because they had struck a deal with the police. The police told them, 'Go put those students down and we'll take care of you.' Twenty rand each, or something. The birth of black-on-black violence. Now it's our greatest problem. It's what the whites use to justify their control of us. They say 'The animals just kill each other, imagine what they'll do if we give them their freedom.' This is a critical time. We can't afford to let one man, Mandela, a professional martyr, have all the power."

He paused for breath. Chanda looked around the room, but the others stayed silent and unmoving.

"You're too smart to waste your life sitting on a barstool. Those damn shebeens are a bigger enemy to black people than every Eugene Terreblanche out there. You know what you learn in the shebeens? You learn to hate yourself, your blackness. Next time you go to Kaiser's or Barcelona, take a look at those old fools you drink with. What have they done with their lives? What are they doing for other people? All they've done is justify everything the whites say and think about us: lazy, drunk, out of work, ignorant. You want to see yourself on one of those stools in thirty years?"

David looked at his watch. "I've got to go. Think about this, then come see me again. If you want to walk away, I won't hold it against you. But you'll regret it. This is your chance to do something that matters. Walk with me."

They walked outside. Chanda heard the others begin to stir and mumble in the dark room behind them.

"I heard about your father. I'm sorry."

Chanda nodded. "I remember what you said about the mines."

"It's true. Your father worked hard. He died because of someone else's mistake, or bad conditions. But nobody will pay for it. The mine owners don't care, because the people who die are powerless."

"It's a fucking joke," Chanda said.

David smiled at him, then walked alone for several paces. "We'll talk again soon," he said. Steve Lekoelea and two others came from the shanty and jogged after David, and they flanked him as he walked rapidly and with purpose down the rutted street.

46

Over the next week Bornwell gave three presentations to children at the community center. At first he was nervous and awkward, and when the kids misbehaved or asked irrelevant questions — one of them repeatedly asked Bornwell to flex his arm muscles — he panicked and waited for Sara to step in and restore order.

He soon settled down, and the kids sat in rapt attention as he told stories of boomslangs and mambas, and lions that circled in the night. He showed them the films he'd made at Umhlaba — Franz had kept them for him — and the children gasped and cheered at the crocodiles, hyenas, and wild dogs. A few of the children had been to Kruger on sponsored trips, but most of them had seen no more wildlife than a child growing up in Joburg or Durban, and the films he showed and the stories he told convinced them that there was magic in the tangled land to the east.

At night, Bornwell and Sara watched movies on her small television. He had never thought of her as anything other than a casual friend, and he still didn't. But sitting there alone with her, remembering Chanda's teasing, he was sure that he was supposed to be thinking of something else. Certainly Sara didn't seem to find the situation strange or awkward. Mostly she used him as a sounding board, talking about her plans for the center.

"I have great hopes," she said, "and I'm mostly happy, especially when I think about what we might be able to do. But it makes me sad, too."

"What does?"

She shrugged. "All of it. Even the good things. The center will be going full-time soon, and I worry that—that there won't be anything left of me."

"What do you mean?"

She groaned. "Ah, you know. Nothing serious. Just that I won't have any free time."

The phone rang. Sara answered it and handed it to him. "It's Franz."

He took the phone. "Hello, Franz?"

"Hello, Bornwell. Got some news for you. Sabi Sabi want you to come for an interview. I talked to Peter van Himst myself. But they want you to go to the business office, in Sandton. They're a big operation, not like us, so you've got to fill out applications and talk to people there before you meet Peter. But he sounded very interested."

"That's great, great," Bornwell said. "When do they want me there?"

"Ag, they're not bothered. I told them you'd need a few days to wrap up business here. Call them to set it up. How are the presentations going?"

"Good, the children seem to like them. When they pay attention, at least."

"Good for you."

After he hung up, he told Sara the news, and she smiled. "That means you'll be close," she said. "Maybe you can keep coming to the center, once or twice a month."

"I don't have the job yet. But if I get it, I'll come back," he said. "Or even if I don't."

He meant it. But already his thoughts were deep in the bush.

Bornwell walked down the street of his mother's home with the slightly stupefied smile of the returned traveler who can't help wondering why he isn't welcomed home with a parade. When he reached his mother's house, he found it empty. She was still at work, and he no longer had a key. Somewhere during his chaotic travels he'd lost it.

He climbed the fence and tried the back door and all the windows, but found no way in. He stretched out on the lumpy red earth of the tiny backyard and tried to sleep. He was tired from the long bus ride, but could only stare up at the fluttering laundry on the line, and the clear sky, watching it as it blushed from bright, high-veld blue to evening violet. He waited for the stars, but they wouldn't come—he was back in the city. He felt the immensity of the rows of shanties, of Soweto and Johannesburg beyond, and he suddenly realized with a startled panic that he had to get the job at Sabi Sabi.

He finally fell asleep. He dreamed forgettable dreams of

the smokestacks and bent antennae and factories of the city. His mother came home at eight o'clock and had no cause to go in the backyard—the laundry could wait—and so Bornwell slept until the air turned cold and woke him. He stood and rubbed his bleary face and saw the light in the house and his mother standing in the kitchen. He called to her and she smiled hugely and ran to the front door. He called again: "I'm in the back!"

She laughed and ran to him, throwing her full arms around his haggard shoulders. "Where have you been? Don't think I was worried, no! But you should have called more."

"I called as much as I could."

They went inside, and Bornwell told her about Cape Town and the camping and the possible job at Sabi Sabi. She was tired, and soon went to bed, but Bornwell was refreshed from his backyard nap. He went to the small room that was his alone and looked through his study books until road weariness overcame him again. Before he fell asleep, he noticed on the table next to his bed a small piece of paper—Alex Stanzis's business card. Looking at it carefully, he turned it over and ran his fingertips across the raised ink of the lettering. "Miami, Florida." There were two small palm trees in green ink in the corner.

He turned off the light and went to sleep in his bed in the township of Izolo in Soweto. Now his nighttime chorus was not the hum of insects or the calls of wandering animals, as it had once been—or, more recently, Chanda's snoring—but the churning metallic groan of diesel trucks and laughter from the shebeens.

The next day Bornwell looked for Chanda. First at Kaiser's, and then at the Barcelona shebeen, the old regulars told him the same thing: Chanda was with David now.

Bornwell walked the streets the rest of the day. He saw a Kusasa group on Pfeni Street, but neither David nor Chanda were with them. He went to his house three times, but Chanda wasn't home, and Bornwell didn't have the stomach to deal with Marks and his other hyperactive younger cousins.

Late in the night, Chanda woke him by tapping on his window—his old habit. Bornwell walked outside, and the two cousins sat in the street. The night was windy. Dimly illuminated by the lights of the city, the clouds skirting overhead hung low and tumbled like old, torn newspapers blowing down an empty street.

"The old farts at Kaiser's told me you were hanging around with David," Bornwell said.

Chanda smiled tightly. "You didn't believe it, I hope?"

"I don't know."

Chanda spoke quietly and slowly, staring straight ahead. "Well, I wouldn't say I've joined Kusasa or anything. But I have met with David. I had to—had to face the music. He came to see me as soon as he heard I was back. He wanted me to join him—join Kusasa. I said no. He said then to stay with him for a couple of days and learn what he wants to accomplish, then I can make up my mind." Chanda shrugged. "That's all."

"So you're finished with him now?"

"Well, maybe. He's got a lot of good ideas, really. And he's not a violent person. It's all these goons he's got with him, and he would really like to get rid of them now."

"I don't believe that," Bornwell said.

"It's true, though. That's why he wants me, and others like me, to join him. If he was really interested in just violence, what good would a guy like me be to him?" He picked up a pebble and tossed it into the center of the street. "Anyway, it's not like I have a lot of other options."

Bornwell shook his head. "When we were in Cape Town you were talking about taking that supervisor training program in Kimberley."

"After what happened to my father? Are you kidding?"

"You'll have to do something. Everybody does."

A dog walked down the street in front of them. A man called to the dog from the shadows, but the dog kept walking. Chanda whistled to it, but it jaunted into the darkness.

"I know," Chanda said. "But if I don't find something soon . . ."

Bornwell stood. "I've got to sleep."

9

Chanda did not succumb to David Themba's charisma gradually. It happened instead in just a handful of days. Born followers rarely need much persuasion. He spent long hours with David, smoking grass from David's pipe and listening to him talk to the others. There was no conversation. The others never had anything to say.

It was easy for them to believe in David. He was worldly and had more education than the rest of them combined. A handwritten 11,000-word essay had won him a scholarship to an experimental high school in London when he was seventeen. He hadn't asked to go. His teacher submitted the essay without consulting David. He rarely spoke of his six months there, although he still wore a red Liverpool Football Club sweatshirt sometimes. He once dismissed the English as "nostalgic for their lost empire." Colonization was a frequent topic of his monologues.

"Yeah man, what happened to Africa when the colonies gained independence? All the new countries suffered at first. Incompetence in government. Corruption in government. So the white conservatives use this as proof that black people were better off when they were colonies. They say, 'Look how much better the natives had it when white people were in charge. Look how bad their lives became after we left!' Man, don't be fooled by this bullshit! The only reason life was so bad after colonialism was because during colonialism, the whites never allowed the natives to hold positions of responsibility. The whites bred themselves a race of servile laborers. So, of course, it was a cluster-fuck when the whites left. What else could have happened? How were they supposed to know how to run a country?"

David took a drag from a small joint. "But eventually they learned. They learned in India, they learned in Kenya, they learned in Botswana, and they'll learn here, where the same thing is about to happen." He passed the joint to Chanda. "You understand what I'm saying?" Chanda understood the question was meant for him alone, and he nodded.

"There are two kinds of dissent. There's rhetoric, which is just listing everything that's wrong, bitching about injustice. Rhetoric is fine if it is a starting point, but too often that's all there is. Rhetoric is Chief Buthelezi. Rhetoric is Nelson Mandela. Rhetoric is F.W. de Klerk. Rhetoric is Eugene Terreblanche. Don't be fooled by these elections. The ANC will win, but F.W. has his hand in Mandela's pocket already. Nothing will change—at least not here.

"Then there's the other kind of dissent: magnetic dissent. That's what I'm trying to do—persuade people to join the struggle, to share our goals. Strength in numbers. This is much, much harder. Not many have been successful. Empty slogans and rhetoric don't go far in getting actual followers. Always remember this: whatever form your protests take, make sure they are magnetic, not just rhetorical."

David pointed at Chanda. "ANC will win the election. So what can we do to make it a positive development here?"

Chanda strained for an original thought, but David held up a hand.

"It's okay. There's no easy answer." He beckoned for the joint again, and dragged on it when it came. "The key to any magnetic movement is visibility. People have to see what we stand for to hear our message. Our message is African unity, all black people working together to run the country, with multitribal representation, and special township representatives. Nothing new? Maybe not, but nobody else has tried the magnetic approach."

Chanda examined the other faces in the room. Most of them were older than he was, by several years. If they understood what David was saying, they showed little sign of it.

"The whites built this country," David said solemnly. Then he smiled. "Just like they taught us in school: They built the roads, the schools, the hospitals. Yes, they built them, but it's really hard to find a white man with dirt under his fingernails." A couple of men laughed from the darkness, and David laughed with them. "Ah, our friends the whites. They won't ever go, so forget that thought right now. South Africa has gold and diamonds and other riches, so they aren't leaving, ever. But that doesn't mean they can continue to dominate us. These elections are a step in the right direction. But we have to have more. Visibility — like I was saying before — is the key. The best way to be visible is to be notorious, like the IRA in Ireland. Yes, they are 'terrorists,' but they have a just cause. And in any worthwhile cause, some people get sacrificed. Do you think the IRA would have the same level of visibility if all they did was stage protests and marches and write letters?"

Chanda assumed it was a rhetorical question, but several of the others, eager to make a contribution, said, "No!"

David rolled his eyes. "So we're going to use their example. We'll become notorious, too, then visible, so that more can hear our message. We won't do it just like the IRA — we won't be bombing innocent people. But it will be dangerous. And there won't be time to drink or chase women. We have a just cause. It's time to work. Some of you, I've been

telling you this for months, and you still haven't done anything. Well, this is it: you work now, or get the fuck out.
This is how we'll do it."

David talked for two more hours, outlining his specific
plans to increase Kusasa's visibility. Chanda was troubled
by what he heard, but only a little bit. Mostly he thought
that it was sure to succeed.

The days grew shorter in the high veld, and at night anyone outside found it necessary to pull on a jacket. In Izolo the boys could no longer play soccer in the lanes, because brief but heavy rains had turned them into inextricable mud.

The elections were only two weeks away. The rich whites of the northern suburbs feared black rule for more reasons than they cared to contemplate, and had taken to making dark jokes about their own futures. The mostly-Zulu Inkathas feared repercussions after the inevitable ANC victory. Mine workers in the hostels feared more violence from the frustrated Inkathas. And rural farmers and workers, white and black, had enough problems as it was, trying to work the ungenerous red earth.

In the low veld, the summer seemed to have no end. The bush was still thick with growth. Rangers all over Kruger Park and the private preserves set prescribed burns to clear the ground cover. Natural fires erupted, too, ignited by lightning from late-summer storms. Unseasonal rain had assuaged the drought of recent years, and the Sabie and Olifants Rivers once again ran swollen and brown. The rain was hard on the crocodiles. They had become accustomed to rich hunting in small pockets of the rivers, where the shrinking water had forced all the game to drink. Now the springbok and zebra could find a drink anywhere. But the flat dogs still found the odd careless impala.

For the lions, who needed to eat much more often than crocs, the thin hunting, combined with an outbreak of biting flies in the northeastern Transvaal, made life almost impossible. Tourists were shocked to see bony lions with missing clumps of hair stumbling across the roads. But the lions, too, would find a way to survive.

Bornwell knew this was happening in the bush—he knew what it meant when the rain finally fell. But he didn't know what to make of the headlines he saw in the papers:

TERREBLANCHE INSISTS ON A WHITE HOMELAND
7 KILLED, 27 INJURED AT ANC RALLY
TERREBLANCHE LOYALISTS STORM RADIO STATION, TAKE OVER
PROGRAMMING
MANDELA, BUTHELEZI MEETING CANCELLED
DATE OF ELECTIONS PUSHED BACK—CHAOS FEARED
INKATHAS MARCH ON PRETORIA

In the Eastern Transvaal, Franz decided he would have to close the lodge during the voting, since his entire staff was likely to be gone. He didn't mind. The lodge had been full for weeks, and all the downsizing had actually worked—it had been a strain, but they had saved a lot of money. He could close for a few days, no harm done.

Bornwell found day work and waited for his scheduled interview with Sabi Sabi. He hadn't seen Chanda since his late-night visit. At the shebeens, he heard that Chanda now held a position of importance in Kusasa. "You're his cousin, can't you do something about it?" an old man said to him.

Bornwell thought, I can bring him to his senses before he gets killed.

51

"Chanda, do you remember when I told you I needed your help controlling some of the Kusasa, to keep the thuggery to a minimum?" David said.

"I remember."

David groaned. "Steve. I've had enough of him. I want you to be at the Jabavu School with him next week."

"But I thought you would be there, too."

"No, I don't think so. I'm getting sicker. I need to rest."

"Well, of course I'll go, but have you told Steve yet?"

"You tell him."

Chanda laughed. "Are you crazy? He hates me already."

"Just tell him this is how I want it."

Chanda laughed nervously. "If you say so," he said. He scratched his head and squinted. "What if he—"

"Chanda, Steve sometimes gets carried away. It's important that we don't go overboard. This is a chance to get the community behind us. Nobody likes all the police in the schools. Don't let Steve start a goddamn street war," David said.

"What can I do to stop him? He doesn't listen to me."

"Just stay in his ear. Make him listen. Keep reminding him how I want it done. I want you there just in case something happens to him. The others would need leadership. Without a leader, they're like children. We can't trust them on their own."

Chanda stood, then sat back down. "Wait a minute. Are you saying something is going to happen to Steve?"

David shrugged. "I've planned something. It's better if you don't know the details. But remember, plans don't always work. If you see guns, get out of there fast. Leave Steve and the rest. I'm going to need you."

"What could go wrong?"

"In case you haven't noticed, the police have a history of panicking when confronting organized protests."

"Steve will shoot me if I try to run," Chanda said.

"Then shoot that bastard first."

52

F ive of them sat in the shanty, but it was so dark that only the faintest outlines could be seen slumped in the corners. The air was heavy and still, and a thin wisp of smoke from David's joint curled to the roof. He sat in the center of the room. "Chanda," he said flatly, his voice echoing faintly. There was none of his usual energy behind it. He had been sick for days.

"Yes?"

"Have you finished the book?"

"Yes, David. Here it is." He handed David a well-worn copy of *Facing Mount Kenya* by Jomo Kenyatta.

"What did you think?" David said.

Chanda grimaced. "I'm not sure I understand why you wanted me to read it."

"You didn't like it?"

"No, I did. But I liked the one about Ho Chi Minh better."

"Why?"

"Because he was just a little man, but he beat the French,

and then he beat the Americans. Kenyatta's book didn't have anything to do with revolution or leadership. It was just Kenyatta telling every single detail of Gikuyu life."

"It had everything to do with revolution," David said. "It was about the most important aspect of revolution — culture."

"But how are marriage ceremonies and harvest techniques about revolution?"

David laughed. "Okay, some of it is boring. The harvest techniques, yes, I'd forgotten about that. But what Kenyatta was doing was making a distinction between his culture, Gikuyu, and the culture of the English who were just then colonizing Kenya. The important thing is that he really did know his culture. Not everyone knows the culture they grow up in, but Kenyatta did, and later he used it against the British."

"How?"

"By appealing to his people in a way only someone who knows their culture could understand. See, the English outlawed polygamy. The English outlawed female circumcision. The English instituted Christianity. So Kenyatta said to his people, 'Do you want to know why your crops are bad? Why your children disobey? Why your daughter is ill? Because the British have stolen your gods, your wives, your traditions.' See, Kenyatta was educated, but he didn't try to protest politically or intellectually. That wouldn't have had an impact on the masses, the rural Gikuyu. He spoke their language, he wore the traditional dress, even though he kept Western suits hanging in his closet for when he needed them. He kept saying these things, and he won back the country for his people. It's another reason I need your help, Chanda. Sometimes I forget, the people here haven't had the education I have. They haven't read the books I've read, they haven't seen the world. I expect them to know things that they can't know. I need someone to remind me of that."

Chanda nodded slowly. "I'll help you with that."

"Good. So what do you know about Kenya today?"

Chanda wasn't nervous this time. "They're independent. There's a statue of Kenyatta in Nairobi, and the airport is named after him."

"That's right. But here, so much is still the same as when Kenyatta was a boy. Look at the Zulu people today."

"Today they're grocery clerks and garden boys," Chanda said, picking up David's meaning.

"That's right!" David stood up and gestured around the room. "Listen to him," he said, pointing at Chanda.

"Some of the Inkathas live traditionally," Chanda said, "but not many. The assegais is gone. The spirit is washed from their blood."

"Replaced by Coca-Cola," David said. He smiled and slapped palms with Chanda. "And what do you think Kenyatta would think of that?"

"He'd hate it."

"And who would he blame?" David said.

"The whites!" one of the shadowy figures yelled.

David faced the man. "Don't jump to conclusions. Kenyatta would blame the Zulus themselves. They fell to temptation. Temptation of the white way of life, the toys and cars and money and useless gadgets."

"But they weren't educated properly," Chanda said. "They were educated to think this way by the whites."

David nodded. "Well, you're right about that. But there's still the temptation of the white world, and it's a powerful thing for anyone living in a shanty or a mud hut. We have to eliminate this temptation. That's all we can do to restore our spirit, to stop trying to be like them, or make them love us. There's only one way to eliminate the temptation."

"Eliminate the white man's world?" Chanda ventured, knowing it was ridiculous as soon as he said it.

"Ha-ha! It's good you have ambition, that's a good thing. But eliminating the white man's world, forget it. Not possible. The whites have an important role to play in South Africa's future. We have to admit this much.

"Anyway, we don't have to eliminate the white man. We have to eliminate his influence. We have to eliminate the forces controlling the people. We're already slipping through his fingers, but he's squeezing tighter." He finished his joint and beckoned for another.

"Soon blacks will govern blacks, but it won't be any better, or, at least, not as much better as Mr. Mandela says. The Soviet Communists are leading the ANC by the nose. It won't be a democracy."

Chanda nodded. "I see that."

David dragged on the joint, then handed it to Chanda. "So, now tell me what you think of Kenyatta's book. What did it teach you about us?"

Chanda took the joint and thought for a moment. "We wanted comfort, and it led us to oppression. It was easier to find work in the cities than to stay in the old villages. Now we're soft."

"That's good. That's true. Man, I feel so much better just listening to you talk like this." Chanda nodded, though he felt like hugging David.

They were all silent for a few minutes, until David laughed and said, "Since when are we so serious here? We're just talking, it's not a funeral. Steve, you've got your stereo here? Play some Peter Tosh."

Steve put in a CD, and the room filled with the rumbling syncopated bass of reggae, and David sang with a levity Chanda had never seen in him: "Arise, black man, arise! Arise and know thyself!" He sang a few more verses, then gradually grew somber again. When the song ended, he said, "I've heard that the Azanian People's Front want me dead, for some reason. They're getting numbers together to come for me."

Steve stood up. "If they come, we'll goddamn well fight!" he said.

David shook his head. "That will leave both sides with five live bodies. It's okay. So many things will have happened before they find me. APF could kill me. My sickness will kill me. One way or another, I know I'm going to go. But it isn't going to be like that. I've got a better way." He was silent for a moment. "We've got a weapon they don't—someone who's not afraid to die. That's what will make the difference."

53

Chanda, Steve, and twenty-five other Kusasa stood in front of the secondary school in Jabavu, holding neatly drawn signs that read POLICE OUT and GO WHERE YOU'RE NEEDED — AND WANTED. There had been little resistance from the police, who merely glared at them from the school, and they'd drawn a crowd of onlookers and passed out leaflets David had written. Steve had been cordial to Chanda, even friendly, but Chanda could tell Steve was eager to show the others who was in charge. He shouted slogans and led the growing crowd of onlookers in songs. By noon, the police had had enough. A sergeant crossed the street and approached them.

"You can't obstruct this street," the man said sternly. "Who's in charge here?"

"I am," Steve said, stepping close to the man, looming over him by a foot.

"Listen, son, you have to keep the street open. Sing and dance all you want, but the street stays clear."

"We're here in protest of your presence in our schools. You're not needed and not wanted."

"I don't care why you're here, I just want you out of the street."

"Why do you profane this school? Why do black children have to learn with your guns all around them?" Steve's voice rose and quavered with malice. Chanda leaned toward him. "Take it easy," he whispered.

The sergeant quickly lost his temper. "I'm not arguing policy with you, I'm telling you to keep the street clear!"

"Free schools for Azania!" Steve roared. The sergeant was momentarily startled by the outburst. He shook his head and laughed in derision. "Free schools for Azania!" Steve shouted again, even louder. The other Kusasa and some of the onlookers joined in the shouting, while others, unsure of what to do, smiled at the spectacle.

The sergeant sighed and said, "Keep the street clear and you can sing all day. But there are children inside trying to learn." He started back to the school, but when Steve shouted "White pigs out of Jabavu!" he turned and put his hand on his revolver.

"David doesn't want confrontation today," Chanda whispered to Steve.

"I know what David wants," Steve said.

The sergeant spoke in Afrikaans on his radio, and six officers ran from the school and joined him. They walked toward Steve and Chanda. The Kusasa men had been spread across the street, and as the police approached, they instinctively coalesced in a tight pack.

"This little demonstration is over," the sergeant said. "I told you to clear the street. You didn't. You can disperse right now, or you can keep standing there, and in ten seconds every one of you will be arrested."

The Kusasa shuffled and swayed, waiting to follow Steve's example. The sergeant began counting in a loud voice. Steve said, "We stay!"

"No, we go," Chanda said calmly. He turned to the other Kusasa. "We go now."

Steve whirled. "What do you think you're doing? Nobody moves! Who the hell put you in charge?"

"David did," Chanda said. "Isn't that right?" he said to the other Kusasa. Steve turned to them. Some of them refused to meet his eyes, but others nodded, and a few said, "That's right."

By now the sergeant had counted to ten. Chanda faced the Kusasa men and said, "We're done here." This time the men turned and began walking away from the school. Chanda and Steve were left facing each other. The sergeant, from behind Steve's back, gestured to Chanda in a way he didn't understand. The sergeant pointed at Steve and mouthed the word "Him?" Now Chanda suddenly understood. He nodded at the sergeant and stepped back. Steve sensed something was up. He turned to the stony face of the sergeant, then back to Chanda.

"I'm sorry, man," Chanda said. "David appreciates everything you've done for him, but he feels you've gotten out of control." Chanda nodded again to the sergeant, who placed a hand on Steve's shoulder. "How about coming with us, lad," the sergeant said.

Steve looked in confusion at Chanda. "This was all a setup?" he said.

Chanda shrugged. "David told you how he wanted things run. You wouldn't listen to him."

Steve lunged at Chanda and swung a meaty right fist at him. Chanda narrowly ducked it, and the police quickly tackled Steve and cuffed his wrists behind his back. Chanda watched them lead Steve away. He felt sorry for the big stupid man, but he was glad to be rid of him. Now they could get something done.

He joined the rest of the Kusasa and immediately noticed they were looking at him differently. They waited until he walked to the front of the group, then followed him.

There was a sudden rainstorm in Izolo, and the alleys and streets ran red as the earth washed away. The children who were bouncing on discarded bedsprings ran for cover. Soweto children are masterful improvisers. Old bedsprings became trampolines. Rags stuffed in a T-shirt substituted for soccer balls. Discarded fence posts worked fine as cricket bats. But the rain was cold, so the bedsprings would wait.

The children huddled underneath a tin roof. A figure walked by. The children pointed and laughed. Didn't he know to get out of the rain, as cold as it was?

Bornwell took little notice of the rain. He bent to it and tightened his weatherproof bush jacket against his neck. He walked all that day and much of the next, all over Izolo, but he didn't see Chanda or, in fact, any Kusasa at all. He went to Kaiser's and the Barcelona shebeen, to see if anyone had heard where Chanda might be—and in the Barcelona he found Chanda himself sitting alone at the bar.

"Bornwell! I was wondering where you've been."

They shook hands. "No new job yet?" Chanda said.

"I'm still waiting on Sabi Sabi. I'm supposed to interview. I guess you've got a new job, from what I hear."

Chanda laughed. "No, it's not a job. A job is work you do for someone else, usually unwillingly, for money. That's not what we do."

"Which is?"

"We work for ourselves. And for everyone in the townships."

Bornwell sat down. "I don't get it. Just a few weeks ago we were running for our lives from these guys, and now you're one of them."

Chanda laughed. "It's true, we ran like a couple of scared rabbits. I'm glad, too—it was fun, and I got to see the country. But that was all Steve, and we've—well, we've taken care of Steve now. And David says that if you want to be a ranger, be a ranger. He means you no harm."

"All these years you've called him crazy, and now you're ready to dedicate your life to him?"

Chanda shrugged. "Yeah. The thing is, I never really knew him."

"But what good do you think is going to come from this? How are you going to make a living? Or is David going to take care of you forever?"

"Making a living is nothing. It's trivial. You having a beer?"

Bornwell said, "Sure, I guess." He ordered two beers from the bartender, but Chanda said, "No, a lemonade for me." When the bartender brought them their drinks, Chanda said, "No more beer for me."

Bornwell sipped his beer and brooded. Chanda tried to talk to him about Pirates, about girls, but Bornwell couldn't concentrate. He kept bringing up David until Chanda interrupted him.

"Bornwell, have you ever thought that maybe what you want for me isn't what I want for me?"

"Maybe, so what? I don't trust what you want."

"And I'm supposed to trust what you want for me? You want me to get a good job, get married, have a family, right?"

"The job part is a good idea. I haven't thought ahead to the rest of your life—wife and family, that stuff."

"Sure you have. Be honest. What sort of chance do you think I have for that kind of life? We both know—zero chance. There's only one future for me in your world—down the mines."

Bornwell started to protest, but Chanda interrupted him again. "You know it's true. I don't have any special skills, like you do. I'm not a very hard worker. I'd never be one of those fellows who works his way up from the bottom. I'd start at the bottom, and I'd stay there. The bottom of a mine shaft, dead before I'm fifty, like most of them." He swigged from his lemonade. "Just like my father."

Bornwell banged his beer bottle in frustration on the bar. "What makes getting mixed up with Kusasa any better? You think you'll live longer that way?"

"Maybe not longer, but better. I'll be making my own decisions, instead of being a victim. And I might make things a little better for the people around me. David gave me that option. You, man, your world, don't give me any options."

Bornwell stood up. "Whatever the fuck, I don't know. You do what you want."

Chanda laughed. "You don't mean that. You've always expected me to do what you want. But that's okay." He finished his lemonade. "I've got to go meet David right now. Why don't you come with me? He'll be happy to talk with you. Then, when you judge us, at least you'll know what you're talking about."

Bornwell shook his head. "I don't have anything to say to him."

"Suit yourself." He dropped a few bills on the table. "You can walk with me for a few minutes, anyway."

They walked out of the bar together. The rain had stopped, but it was still chilly. Chanda wasn't dressed for it. "Damn," he said, rubbing his arms. They walked together for a long time. Bornwell didn't want to leave Chanda. They walked across the vacant lot where the kids played soccer, splashing across the muddy ground, and old men sat drinking and laughing. They stepped around puddles of mud. The sky darkened over the hills of Izolo, and a chorus of whistles cascaded from the shanties as mothers called their children to supper.

Chanda stopped suddenly and put his hand on Bornwell's shoulder. "We're still friends," he said. "But I can't go along with everything you say anymore. This is important to me. It's what I want to do. I want to be involved."

"Isn't there a safer way to be involved?"

"Safer? It's not about safety. I don't want safety, I don't want comfort. I want equal rights. I want justice."

They walked some more, until Chanda said, "We're here."

"David lives here?" They stood in front of an abandoned store with no glass in the windows.

"He moves around a lot. Come talk to him."

Bornwell shook his head. "It's not for me. You know that."

"I know. You're very lucky, Bornwell. You've always known what you wanted. Most people have no idea. I've had to make it up as I've gone along. You should remember that."

Bornwell nodded. "Okay." He brushed raindrops out of his hair. "I'd better get home." He awkwardly patted Chanda on the shoulder. "Go well, Chanda."

"Stay well, Bornwell."

He watched Chanda disappear into the dim structure. He heard a voice formally greet him. The wind changed direction, and the rain blew into his face. He turned his back to it and walked home.

55

Those who had wood stoves burned them at night and in the mornings now. The skies were clear and blue during the day, and the air was mild, but at night the winds blew from the cold, dry west. Soweto huddled behind tin and plywood, with rocks on the tin roofs to keep them from blowing away in the winter winds. But the roofs were thin, and sometimes the rocks fell through.

Bloodshed continued in Natal. Rival gangs, organized along ANC and IFP lines, clashed. In many regions the police gave up and local citizens evacuated. Soweto was placid by comparison, although everyone bristled with the anticipation of voting. Bornwell, though, was still trying to get a job.

The time of his interview with Peter van Himst of Sabi Sabi had arrived. Bornwell wore his only suit. He felt silly sitting in a crowded minivan in his finest clothes. Two young boys sitting across from him kept giggling and staring at him. Finally one of them said, "Are you Marks Maponyane?"

Bornwell released his tension in a raucous laugh. "Marks Maponyane, who plays for Pirates? I wish!"

"I told you!" said one boy to his friend.

"Well he looks like him still," said the other.

He was nervous during the interview and fumbled his words more than once. Nonetheless, Peter seemed pleased with him and promised that Bornwell would be hearing from him soon. But there was something in the man's eyes when he said it—a flicker of pity, perhaps—that made Bornwell think he'd blown it.

Vaguely disheartened, Bornwell went to the house in the Bryanston suburbs where his mother worked as a maid. He had spent many boyhood afternoons there, playing with the dogs and stalking lizards as they stalked ants. But when he turned twelve, the Hartleys, who had a daughter Bornwell's age, told Mrs. Malaba to leave her son at home. The daughter evidently was "scared" of Bornwell. Bornwell couldn't recall the girl saying more than a handful of words to him over the years, and didn't understand why he was no longer allowed to play in the yard.

Later, when Mrs. Malaba told the Hartleys that Bornwell was an apprentice ranger at Umhlaba, they visited the lodge. There they greeted Bornwell as if he were a long-lost relative, and insisted he visit the house the next time he was in Johannesburg. He never got around to it.

He walked from the Sabi Sabi office to the Bryanston suburbs. All he could see of the houses from the streets were the roofs. It wasn't how he remembered it. Now, most northern suburb houses crouched behind huge walls topped by either electric fencing or barbed wire. Razor wire—effective and relatively aesthetic—was the current favorite.

Bornwell walked past these fortresses until he came to the Hartleys' house on Coventry Lane. He pushed the call button outside the gate. A wary, crackly voice said, "Who is it?"

"Bornwell, Dorothy's son."

"Bornwell, yes, just a moment." The gate hummed to life and rolled open. Mrs. Hartley walked out of the house and smiled. She was a bony, angular fossil of a woman who clung to the notion that she was a glamorous beauty — as indeed she'd once been — despite considerable evidence to the contrary. She waltzed down her cobblestone driveway in an immaculate white tennis outfit and extended her hand.

"So good to see you again! How are things at the lodge?"

"I'm no longer working there, but I've just come from an interview with Sabi Sabi."

"Ah, what a shame. Well, your mother is in the courtyard. You can go in."

He walked around the back of the house and entered the little courtyard where his mother did the washing. She was hanging bedsheets on the clothesline and clasped her hands to her chest when she saw Bornwell. "It went well, didn't it? I can tell from your face," she said.

"Uh — yes. I think the man liked me. Plus I've got Franz's recommendation."

"We shouldn't get our hopes too high, but it sounds good. When will you know?"

"Soon. This week or next."

She nodded. "Can you stay and visit? I have to keep working, because I've fallen behind, but you can talk to me."

They talked for an hour before Mrs. Hartley stuck her head out the courtyard window and said, "Dorothy, can I have your help in the kitchen?" Bornwell said good-bye and walked down the driveway toward the gate. Mrs. Hartley trotted out after him. "I'll walk you out, I have to get my mail." He waited for her in the driveway, and together they walked to the gate.

"I can remember when you used to run around here after lizards," she said. "It seems like yesterday, but it must be fifteen years ago."

"I remember, too. You still have lots of lizards."

She smiled and laughed, and Bornwell noticed how she had aged, how the lines erupted from the corners of her eyes.

"I'm so glad you haven't gotten mixed up in politics like so many of the others your age," she said. "I don't see why they want to change everything overnight. Things have always worked well, why change now? We've always taken good care of the black people who've worked for us. Your mother is practically one of the family, and the van Houtens couldn't get by without their Minah."

"Yes, ma'am."

She groaned. "I suppose I'm just old and like things to stay the same. I think de Klerk has the right idea—change, but change gradually. Mr. Mandela, he wants it all too quickly, because he's old, you see? Oh, he's old, he has no time to wait." She nodded emphatically. She smelled of gin. Bornwell looked at the gate and wished she would push the button on her remote control to open it.

"This 'One man one vote.' How can you vote on issues like education and taxes if you can't read? It makes no sense. You've been educated, you know better."

"Yes . . ."

"They say the lines are going to be so long that the stations will close before many people even get inside." She nodded again, and finally pushed the button. The gate rolled open.

"It's changed here. All the gates and walls and wire," Bornwell said.

"Yes, it's sad. There has been at least one break-in a month, just on our street and the next." She gestured across the neighborhood. "It's not only robberies. Some of them come in to kill and rape. We tried hiring a private armed-guard force here, and the break-ins doubled. Turned out, the guards were in league with the criminals. They even let them into a couple of houses, when they knew nobody was home."

"I've heard of that," Bornwell said. "Terrible."

"Modern life. Now, Bornwell, if you ever need work, you come back here. Mr. Hartley always needs help in the garden."

"Thank you, but as I said, I've just had interviews with Sabi Sabi and should be starting there soon."

"Of course, but we never know what the future holds, isn't that so?"

In South Africa, in 1994, that was especially so.

56

The gentle rapping on his window was familiar. "Chanda?" Bornwell said.

"Come outside," Chanda whispered.

It was three in the morning, just about the regular time for Chanda to wake him with catastrophic news. "What is it?" Bornwell said, meeting Chanda in front of the house.

"Got something for you." Chanda held up two stubs of paper. "Cup semifinal, Swallows versus Jomo Cosmos."

Bornwell shook his body to force himself awake. "Wow. I was going to try to go to the Pirates-Spurs game, but everyone says there are no tickets for that one."

"Well, yeah. Thing is, you don't want to go to that game."

"Why not?"

"David has heard that the APF—that's a political gang, a rival—are planning a demonstration. There's an ANC rally after the match. David thinks it's going to be something big, something really violent."

"Are you going?" Bornwell said.

"Just for the match. We aren't staying for the rally."

Bornwell nodded. "I can't afford tickets anyway. I'll take these though, for sure." Chanda handed him the tickets. Bornwell sighed. "So, tell me, what's really going to happen tomorrow?"

Chanda smiled. "We are men of honor, we mustn't deceive each other," he said, then laughed. "Okay, yeah, there's going to be trouble. Nothing too dangerous. Just a demonstration."

"Kusasa is going to demonstrate during an APF demonstration right before an ANC rally. Sounds terrific." They both laughed, but tensely. "Incidentally, you know you can come over before midnight. Why do you always have to wake me in the middle of the night?"

"Oh, I don't know. Maybe because you don't have the energy to lecture me so much. Or maybe I think you look funny when you've been asleep, with lines from your pillow pressed into your face." He laughed softly. "Stay away from that Pirates game," he said, then stood and stretched his arms above his head. "Bound to be a good game, though," he said over his shoulder as he walked away. "Maponyane's knee is finally better."

57

Ellis Park was built to be the home of the Springboks, South Africa's powerful national rugby team that perennially challenged New Zealand, England, and Australia for world rugby dominance. But the stadium saw little of the action for which it was intended, as worldwide condemnation of apartheid in the 1980s led to the boycotting of sporting events involving South Africa. Other countries refused to compete against the Springboks, and Ellis Park, built for rugby, the bastion of white society, became instead the centerpiece for the National Football League's most important games. On these occasions, the sparkling stadium filled with tens of thousands of blacks from the townships—a scene the stadium's architects certainly never intended.

Lately it had become a home to political rallies, as it was this day for the African National Congress, following Pirates' comprehensive 3–1 win over Cape Town Spurs. Over fifty thousand flag-waving ANC supporters filled the stadium and flooded the kelly-green playing field as soon as the soccer game ended. The bright sun tempered the chill of the air. Chanda stood as close to the hastily erected speaker's platform as he could get, surrounded by a landscape of smiling faces singing *"Nikosi sikelel iAfrika."* The song echoed and rang through the stadium, and when it was over, the crowd, patiently awaiting their next president, sang it again.

The platform rose six feet above Chanda's head. Guards toting automatic weapons stood shoulder to shoulder on the ground around the platform. More guards stood along the edge of the platform. Looking at them, Chanda had his first misgivings about David's plan. The guards were alert and nervous. But Chanda noticed the real guards were the ones on the ground. The guards on the platform appeared to be purely ceremonial. They had rifles, but old ones, some with colorful ribbons tied around them.

Nelson Mandela was going to speak, but he hadn't yet arrived. Nor had Cyril Ramaphosa or any of the other ANC leaders. The crowd was being entertained by a singer, a strong-looking man with a voice like a cannon. David had said that when Mandela showed up, the security force would triple in size.

Chanda picked out a few Kusasa faces in the flowing crowd near the platform. They made their way toward him. Each one sidled close and passed him a small rubber flask. Chanda hid them under his coat. After thirty minutes he had been visited by eighteen Kusasa, some of whom he'd never seen before. David must have recruited them that morning.

Each time he was given a flask, he unscrewed the top of a one-gallon plastic jug hidden under his coat and poured the contents inside. The jug was bulky, but people in the crowd were dancing and singing and drinking wine from similar jugs, so no one paid him any attention. He probably could have walked right in with a full jug and told the security guards at the gate it was wine. But David had insisted on every precaution.

Now his gallon jug was full. He felt the liquid slosh when dancers bumped him. He moved as close to the left corner of the stage as he could get. There, for the first time today, he saw David. He was standing ten feet to Chanda's left, talking to some of the armed guards ringing the platform. He patted one of them on the shoulder and handed him a cigarette. He caught Chanda's eye and flashed him a "peace" sign, which meant "We do it in two minutes."

Chanda began to sweat. What if they failed? he thought. What if, God forbid, they succeeded? In two more minutes . . . There were television cameras everywhere, just as David had hoped.

He reached inside his jacket and, with a tiny penknife, began carefully sawing a large opening into the top of the jug. The sweet, rich smell of gasoline wafted up his collar, and he tightened his grip on the handle. He stared at David. David continued chatting pleasantly with the guards. Chanda wondered what he was thinking in these moments. At least David could no longer have any misgivings about his future. Chanda's future was as uncertain as it could be, but David's was absolute.

The guards on the platform stood behind a railing. The platform extended five feet beyond the railing. This is where they would do it, David had said. The guards would have to climb the railing to get to him, and the time it would take would be all the time he would need.

David looked at Chanda and nodded. "There's Mandela," he said to the guards, and the instant they turned their heads, he flashed between them. He put both hands on the platform and vaulted himself onto it and dashed to the spot directly in front of Chanda. The singer was finishing a song, and the crowd was cheering, and the guards didn't notice the figure on the platform, or perhaps they simply thought he was an enthusiastic fan. In any case, they were slow to respond—Mandela was not yet in the stadium, no cause for alarm.

As soon as David reached the platform in front of him, Chanda opened his coat. Suppressing the urge to flee into the crowd, an urge he had known would come at this moment, he doused David with the gasoline from his jug. The gasoline seemed to travel through the air very slowly; Chanda watched it form a graceful amber arc in front of the darkening sky. For a terrible moment, he thought he had missed. But his aim was true. David stood with his legs splayed and unfurled a banner above his head. David had paid for the banner to be professionally painted, and it read KUSASA — FOR AFRICANS in red letters. One of the new Kusasa recruits burst through the crowd next to Chanda. He had balled up a piece of paper and set it on fire, and now he threw it at David. It struck David on the shoulder, and his overcoat, heavy with gas, crackled into soft-blue flame.

It had taken three seconds. Now the guards moved to react, but the flames began raging, and they stepped back. The singer had finished his song and stood in shock, as did hundreds of people near the stage. But much of the crowd in the stadium could not see what was happening. They saw only fire on the stage and thought it was part of the show.

Chanda knew he should start running, but he was struck by David's face. As the fire consumed his clothing and leapt onto his neck and face, he screamed in pain, his eyes squeezed shut, and his mouth spread in a wide grimace. His teeth looked unusually white. The pungent odor of gasoline and burning clothes sat heavy in the air. The banner caught fire and blackened. David's arms quivered, but his back remained straight, and his legs stayed firmly planted. It had been ten seconds, and now he was burning, and everybody saw it.

On television the announcers were shouting, but on stage nobody reacted. Afraid the burning man would topple over on them, the crowd pushed away from the stage, and Chanda finally came to life. He dropped the jug and pushed his way through bodies, remembering David's words to him that morning: "Whatever happens, you get out safe."

Bornwell had given away Chanda's tickets and gone to Kaiser's in order to watch the Pirates game on TV. He heard the announcers shout "He's burning himself!" He saw the figure and read the banner before it blackened. He leapt from his stool and rushed to the television, ignoring the howls and shouts of the others in the bar. He knew it wasn't Chanda—the burning figure was too frail and emaciated.

At Ellis Park all was oddly calm. The burning figure had finally crumpled to the stage, dead. The guards smothered the fire, covered the body with a canvas tarp, and dragged it off the back of the platform. An ANC official announced that all was well, that it had merely been an insignificant extremist group looking for attention on a grand scale. Buckets and mops appeared, the stage was scoured clean, and the wind carried the soot and smell of gas and burnt flesh away from the stadium. The band reassembled, the singer resumed his singing, and the crowd cheered and sang along.

Chanda had no problems slipping out of the stadium. A few Kusasa men were arrested, because they continued to stare at David as he burned, but the others all escaped with Chanda.

When Chanda got out of the stadium, he was shaking violently. He sat on the curb and tried to still his spinning head. He felt faint. But this was the critical time, the one David had warned him about so often. So he stood and walked, bent at the waist and watching his feet, forcing them on.

58

News reports the next day identified the man as David Themba. He was the leader, formerly, of a political group called Kusasa, which recently had been involved in an altercation with police at a school in Jabavu.

So the reports said. And it was over, just like that.

Two days later Bornwell found a letter in his mailbox. It had been hand-delivered.

Bornwell —

As things are now, I won't be able to see you for a long time. I won't be living with my family anymore, either. It's for the best for everyone. David has left me a lot of work. He made the ultimate sacrifice, so what I have to do is pretty easy in comparison. He has written a very brilliant manuscript, and I have to find a publisher for it, among other things. It's about the time he spent in England several years ago—a lot of political stuff that would really bore you to death! But we've made enemies now. It's a dangerous situation, and I don't want you to be involved. I know you don't approve, but I have something to fight for now and I'm going to give myself over to it. Stay well.

Always your cousin and friend,
Chanda

Bornwell wrote a short note in response.

Chanda,

I know you'll do what you have to do. So I say then, do it. Please be careful. Your cause has its martyr now, so it doesn't need another one.

Yes—always your cousin and friend
Bornwell

Bornwell folded the letter and placed it on his table, where it remained for a long time. There was no address for Chanda now.

59

The morning felt fine, and even though the sun had not yet risen, it was not too cold. Dawn came and washed away the stars. It would be warm today, which was good. They would stand in line for a long time.

His mother woke him, and, as he dressed, she prepared a basket of food. They left the house at five, Bornwell carrying the basket and humming along as his mother sang in a high-pitched, morning-unfriendly voice. They walked all the way through Izolo, and the streets that would normally be sleeping were filled with people. Morning fires had already been put out. People emerged from shanties, happy and alert despite the early hour. As they got closer, and the streets became more crowded, spontaneous singing began. Soon they reached a spot where uniformed officials directed the masses of people to form a single line, and this stretched for miles through the townships, though Bornwell and his mother couldn't see this. The officials blew their whistles and motioned vigorously to keep people in line, but the officials were smiling and even joined in the songs that arced from the crowds.

When the sun rose, they still had not moved, but nobody complained. Somewhere in the inconceivable distance ahead of them, gates were opened, and the serpentine miles of humanity took their first tiny, shuffling steps. All over the city and the country, there were lines. The first day of voting had finally come.

As he stood in line, Bornwell thought about Mrs. Hartley. This was going to be a long day, but he was glad to be there.

The day dragged on and brought problems. The line moved imperceptibly — up front, at the voting centers, there was confusion and delay. Some in line let their impatience and temper get the best of them, but most accepted it with good cheer. Helicopters whined overhead. Bornwell thought they carried soldiers or police, keeping watch on them, but the helicopters belonged to international television crews, and live pictures of the unbelievably long lines of people were flashing around the world at that moment.

Bornwell and his mother waited most of the day. In the afternoon it became hot, and he worried about her, but the woman had worked hard all her life and wasn't troubled by standing in the sun. At long last they reached the voting station, though there was still a great deal of waiting even there. When it was their turn, his mother turned to him with an odd expression on her face. She started to speak but stopped herself, then laughed. Bornwell put an arm around her and then led her to the voting booth. When she came out she was quiet, and she waited for Bornwell outside.

"What was it you were going to say back there, Mother?" he said when he joined her.

"It was nothing. A silly thing."

"No, tell me."

She considered the ground at her feet as they walked home, then said, "I had something I was going to say. But you'll get to live with this memory a lot longer than me, and you already have enough to remember. So why add more words?"

They walked home under the canopy of helicopters.

60

In the low veld the dry season began. The days were mild, but at night it was very cold, and some mornings there was frost on the leaves of the camelthorns and jackalberries. The bush began to wither and thin. Despite the summer rains, the rivers were low again, and herds of zebra, wildebeest, and impala congregated at the pools of the Sand River. Hunting was again easy for the flat dogs. They forged a tentative truce with the hippos—beasts of the pools. Lions hid in the bush.

A place of danger. But the animals had to drink.

It was so close—just a dozen miles away. From the steps of the Bosbokrand Community Center, Bornwell could see the sloping hills of the Timbavati, and just beyond this, Kruger Park. He could visit any time, but most days he was too busy to think about it. He worked for the de Wit family during the mornings. He'd started in the garden, but when they realized he was smart and capable, they moved him to the stable, where he took care of their horses. It wasn't hard work, but he had to be there before sunrise every day. He spent the afternoons and evenings at the center. Sara's plan was for Bornwell to take the children on regular trips into Kruger, so they needed to raise money to buy an old Land Rover. It was slow going. In the first three weeks, they raised only three hundred rand.

"Can you even imagine how much better it will be?" Sara kept asking him. "Taking these kids there, teaching them, instead of tourists?"

All he wanted was to get back to the bush. But she was right: this way, it would be better.

61

In Izolo the streets still run red when it rains, and in the mornings you can smell cooking fires under burbling pots of mealie-meal. Outside the Barcelona shebeen, you can find sprawling men who had no place to sleep after the bar closed. Flattened paper cups lie all around them. At the Jabavu school the police keep watch, and young men still gather to insult them from a distance.

Chanda lives in Izolo, but also in Kliptown and Mandelaville and many other places. He no longer sleeps very much, and when you talk to him, you notice how he looks back at you right in the eyes, and never interrupts even if he disagrees, and thinks for a moment before he responds. He doesn't sit inside and read and talk, like David did, but walks every day and talks to people he does not know. Sometimes in the evenings you can see him looking to the east, across the waving corn, across the tin roofs and mines and factories. To the east, past the Drakensburg Mountains, beyond the patchwork farms and furrowed soil heavy with basalt, where the land falls and is hot most of the year, where the sun streams onto bleached bones, and hooves and claws scratch into the baked clay. Bornwell is there, so it's good. They miss each other, but there's no reason to be sad.

It has been two years.

He hasn't seen Pirates play in that time, or had a beer. He has work to do.

The streets run red, and his days as a child are over.

ENC Press
www.encpress.com

Yevgheniy Zamyatin
WE: A XXI-CENTURY TRANSLATION

The first dystopia ever, it started asking uncomfortable questions about individuals, collectives, revolutions, progress — and the collectives' rights to individuals' souls in the name of revolutions and progress.

More info: encpress.com/WE.html

Olga Gardner Galvin
THE ALPHABET CHALLENGE

The big business of organized professional compassion has too much caring to do to care much for the amateur individualists . . .

More info: encpress.com/ABC.html

Mark Mandell
DIARY OF A XX-CENTURY ELIZABETHAN POET

A comedy of manners about an oversheltered, pompous young poet who experiences a culture shock upon falling in love with a fair, albeit slightly worn-out, maiden from a South Florida trailer park.

illustrated gift edition
More info: encpress.com/DXX.html

ENC Press
www.encpress.com

CRAIG FORGRAVE
DEVIL JAZZ

How would mankind react to an alien named Armageddon suddenly stepping into the media spotlight and offering the world a new explanation of the origins of civilization? In New York, in the 21st century, things can go either way.

More info: encpress.com/DJ.html

DAVID GUREVICH
VODKA FOR BREAKFAST

A saga of love, friendship, life, drugs, and opportunities almost lost on an ex-KGB company man who leads a seemingly decent immigrant's life of quiet desperation in New York.

More info: encpress.com/VFB.html

MICHAEL ANTMAN
CHERRY WHIP

An eccentric young Japanese jazz artist, obsessed with new sensations and new experiences, arrives for a career-making gig in New York City, where his quirky adventures are abruptly overshadowed by illness, guilt, and betrayal.

More info: encpress.com/CW.html

ENC Press
www.encpress.com

ANDREW HOOK
MOON BEAVER

Packed with wisecracks, cynicism, and naive hope, *Moon Beaver* examines the meaning of "self" in a society where individuality is a commodity and wasted lives are commonplace.

More info: encpress.com/MB.html

SARAH CRABTREE
TERROR FROM BEYOND MIDDLE ENGLAND

Small-town temp saves the world in this tale about friends, lovers, dysfunctional families, genetic modification, and all kinds of weird stuff that nobody expects to stumble across in a prim and proper English town.

More info: encpress.com/TFBME.html

BETH ELLIOTT
DON'T CALL IT "VIRTUAL"

A coven of time-traveling lesbian activists find themselves in the Alta California Republic in 2064 and realize that the future ain't what it used to be . . .

More info: encpress.com/VSF.html

ENC Press
www.encpress.com

LIAM BRACKEN
EXIT ONLY

A suspenseful, multihued novel of Saudi Arabia as it's seen through the eyes of expatriates of various origins and social standings who have one thing in common: they are all leaving it on the same plane hurtling toward its destiny.

More info: encpress.com/EO.html

COMING SOON

ANDREW THOMAS BRESLIN
MOTHER'S MILK

Yes, there is a secret global conspiracy and at its black heart is a white liquid secreted by extraterrestrial bovines.

More info: encpress.com/MM.html

MARK A. RAYNER
THE AMADEUS NET

Wolfgang Amadeus Mozart is alive and in love, living in the world's first sentient city, Ipolis. Lucky for both of them nobody knows, but how long can it stay that way?

More info: encpress.com/AN.html

ENC Press
www.encpress.com

DAVID A. BRENSILVER
EXECTV

Fast-forwarding Reality TV to its logical extreme, an unemployed documentary filmmaker extraordinaire arranges to have an execution broadcast live on pay-per-view television, in as flamboyant a form as his bizarre vision can conjure to amuse the masses.

More info: encpress.com/TV.html

CHRISTOPHER LARGEN
JUNK

A riotous exploration of prohibition policies, told through the narrative lens of a future America in which the government outlaws junk food in response to widespread obesity.

More info: encpress.com/JUNK.html

MIKHAIL BULGAKOV
A THEATRICAL NOVEL: Journal of a Dead Man

A wretched novelist-turned-playwright helplessly looks on as his play is mangled by a prestigious theater in this sad and viciously funny 1937 satire of Konstantin Stanislavsky and his world-famous Moscow Art Theater.

More info: encpress.com/TN.html

ORDER FORM

If you prefer ordering through the mail rather than through the Internet, you can send this form, along with a USPS money order or a personal check (drawn on a U.S. bank) for the appropriate amount, to

ENC Press
P.O. Box 833
Hoboken, NJ 07030

Your order will be shipped as soon as the payment clears. (Sorry, we cannot accept foreign checks and money orders.)

PLEASE PRINT CLEARLY

Your name _____

Your address _____

_____

Your e-mail address _____

Please check the title(s) you would like to purchase:

		ENC price	Qty.	TOTAL
☐	We	$14		
☐	Don't Call It "Virtual"	$18		
☐	The Alphabet Challenge	$15		
☐	Vodka for Breakfast	$16		
☐	Diary of a XX-Century Elizabethan Poet	$18		
☐	Season of Ash	$15		
☐	Devil Jazz	$14		
☐	Moon Beaver	$16		
☐	Terror From Beyond Middle England	$16		
☐	Exit Only	$18		
☐	Cherry Whip	$15		
☐	Mother's Milk	$16		

S&H 1st book	$3.50
S&H each add'l book	$2.00
sales tax (NJ only)	6%

TOTAL AMOUNT ENCLOSED $